PRAISE FOR SINKING
BOOK ONE OF THE SINKING TRILOGY

"*Sinking* drew me in right from the start with its elegant writing style and perfect blend of history, romance, folklore, and mystery. I loved seeing Jocelyn grow as a character as clues from her past fell into place, and I can't wait to find out what the next book has in store!"

—Laurie Lucking, author of *Common*

"*Sinking* is a beautifully spun tale, sure to entice the most avid fans of mermaids, historical fiction, and romance. It combines adventure, mystery, and a gorgeously created world into an exciting tale that leaves you wanting more. I simply couldn't put it down, and I found myself saying 'Just one more chapter' several times each sitting. I can't wait to see what Sarah Armstrong-Garner has brewing next for our mysterious heroine."

—Katrina Sherwood, actress and YouTube vlogger

"Sarah Armstrong-Garner weaves a magical and mysterious tale about a young woman who longs for the sea, despite it almost claiming her life. From the very first page, I was drawn in to Jocelyn's world and transfixed by the beautiful narrative. Armstrong-Garner takes her readers on a journey they won't soon forget. I can't wait to get my hands on the sequel!"

—Jebraun Clifford, winner of ACFW's 2016 Genesis and 2015 First Impressions contests, Young Adult Category

"If you love Ireland, mysterious pasts, or beautiful descriptions, *Sinking* offers all of the above and then some. Sarah Armstrong-Garner takes readers on a journey where the life of land and sea intertwine. You will be left anxious to read the trilogy's next book and continue the journey."

—Lenn Woolston, book blogger at
www.lennwritesblog.wordpress.com

"*Sinking* is a wonderful blend of fantasy, mystery, and intrigue. In *Sinking*, there's also a touch of fairytale, as well as lovely Ireland in the 18th Century. Mermaids have long captivated not only sailors, but also us land-lubbers. And *Sinking* doesn't disappoint. I was captivated by Jocelyn and even a bit worried. Even though she can't remember who she is or where she came from, she's smart and resourceful. I'm happily anticipating the next book!"

—Pam Halter, author of *Fairyeater*

"I absolutely loved this book! It has mystery, mystique, mermaids, and high-seas adventure!"

—Autumn Lindsey, founder of Writer Moms Inc.

DRIFTING

Now Available:

Sinking
Book One of the Sinking Trilogy
Drifting
Book Two of the Sinking Trilogy

Coming Soon:

Rising
Book Three of the Sinking Trilogy

Standalone Novel:

Autumn in Neverland

DRIFTING

Sarah Armstrong-Garner

Mermaids are neat :)

Love2ReadLove2Write Publishing, LLC
Indianapolis, Indiana

© 2018 Sarah Armstrong-Garner

Published by Love2ReadLove2Write Publishing, LLC
Indianapolis, Indiana
www.love2readlove2writepublishing.com

Library of Congress Cataloging-in-Publication Data is on file at the Library
of Congress, Washington, DC.

ISBN-13: 978-1-943788-30-9 (Ebook edition)
ISBN-13: 978-1-943788-29-3 (Paperback edition)
LCCN: 2018939865 (Paperback edition)

This is a work of fiction. Names, characters, incidents, and dialogues are
products of the author's imagination and are not to be construed as real. Any
resemblance to actual events or persons, living or dead, is entirely
coincidental.

Cover Design by Sara Helwe (www.sara-helwe.com)

For my children,
who will rule the sea because they believed they could

CHAPTER 1

Her pulse pounded through the thick waters, echoing back to her. The rising skin between her fingers held an internal flame glowing and burning through the dark sea. Jocelyn's lungs ordered her to gulp the salty ocean, demanding oxygen. She inhaled, letting the salt scratch down her throat, but the pain pushed through her ribs, tearing her flesh. She wrapped her arms around her chest and pulled her knees up, shielding herself.

But she couldn't protect herself from morphing.

The flame danced down her arms, over her stomach, to her legs. She burned like a torch. Her white dress turned to ash against her scorching skin and fluttered in pieces around her. Exposed, Jocelyn hugged her legs closer, but they were not legs anymore. Her inner thighs molded together, fusing the skin that braided to her feet. Her toes pulled apart as a thin layer of skin webbed together and pulled her heel to the back of her ankle. She arched her back as the stretching tendons ached with the force. Small scales rose from her pale skin, shining like yellow diamonds against the inferno inside of her.

Cramping, Jocelyn's muscles forced her to spread her limbs from her core as the last of the transformation burned brighter. Thin, small fins grew from her elbows, and her large tail danced with the slow current of the sea. The water rushed through her, in and out of the gills under her breasts, tickling her tender flesh. Her lungs rejoiced. She breathed in the water again.

The immobilizing spasm released its grip on her body, allowing Jocelyn to have control once more. Her body descended deeper into the ocean. The fire within her faded, taking with it her only light. Her hope. Darkness forced its way around her morphed body.

You are home, the ocean sang to her.

Jocelyn rubbed her hand up her thigh, pressing against her newly acquired scales that scratched her palm. Focusing, her pupils stretched open, pulling away the iris and sclera until thin rings of blue circled the windows to her soul, allowing the elusive light from the depth of the ocean to paint her surroundings.

Lime algae blanketed rocks that scattered across sand. Jocelyn's flukes hit the sea's floor. She tried to kick her tail to swim upward, but her body was deprived of energy to spring her forward. The rest of her body anchored onto the bed of sand as the shadow of Aidan's ship passed over her.

Don't leave me. Please don't go.

Stretching up her webbed hand, Jocelyn reached for the man she loved.

Her head knocked against the ocean floor as her heart began, once again, to beat faster and faster, until the water vibrated the rhythm back to her heavy body. Her stomach turned as it pushed the poison from her, making her vomit.

Jocelyn remembered the half-breed girl in Calcutta, India —Damini's yellow, bulging eyes, waiting for death to come. The girl was doomed from having a mermaid and human as her parents. Once puberty started, her cells divided, fighting against each other to become human or mer-being, creating poison in her system. Jocelyn had breathed the toxins out of Damini and into herself to save the girl, but it was killing her. Benlar, the merman who came to take Jocelyn home, had thrown her overboard in hopes the ocean could heal her.

Jocelyn threw up again. Her stomach contracted, squeezing out every last bit of its contents. Jocelyn bellowed in pain, pulling her tail closer to her chest, as the ship drifted away on the surface of the ocean with the two men who loved her. Who had kept her safe.

For hours, the ocean caressed her skin with its soft current. With nothing left to spew, Jocelyn's stomach rested. She lay there, breathing in the moonlit water.

Jocelyn ran her fingertips over the medallion's warm, embossed skin. She traced the three twisting waves that surrounded the triangle in the center. Her symbol was different than Benlar's, which Aidan had taken from him, imprisoning him on the ship. His medallion spiraled inward like a shell cut in half.

One, she counted, moving her hands to her back and pushing against the pressure of the water.

Two. She raised herself to her hidden knees. Her stomach protested, making her gag. She stopped moving, waiting for her body to heal. Benlar was right; the ocean was restoring her health. She was still weak, but stronger than she'd ever been on land.

Three. Jocelyn swept the water with her opened hands,

pushing up toward the surface. She kicked her tail and shot up through the water. She did it again, fascinated by the momentum from one movement, rushing her body toward the heavens above.

Her head shoved through the barrier of water and sky to nothing but open sea. She spun, searching for the ship, but it was gone. She was alone.

Jocelyn's lungs panted as she began to hyperventilate. She inhaled the water, giving her relief.

"Aidan!" she screamed into the emptiness.

The air burned her eyes. She closed them as tears welled up, soothing the dryness.

Benlar! Jocelyn screamed through her mind.

I'm here. Benlar's voice echoed in her head.

Jocelyn's eyes shot open.

Mli, are you safe?

Jocelyn nodded. A small dot on the edge of the horizon moved past the clouded night sky, exposing the ship's location. Jocelyn focused on it. Sails. Her heart dropped.

Speak to me, Benlar demanded.

She dove under the water, swimming toward the ship.

Benlar? It was easier to communicate underwater with her mind. It was her natural language.

Are you safe? Benlar's deep voice cracked.

Jocelyn could feel his worry as if it were her own. He did not just speak words—he spoke his emotions to her from miles and miles away.

I've transformed, Jocelyn confessed.

Benlar's relief washed through Jocelyn as her body propelled itself through the ocean toward him.

Go deep, Benlar ordered.

No. I'm coming to you. Don't leave me out here.

It's not safe, Mli. I will be fine.

Doubt dropped her stomach. He was lying to her. *Don't lie to me.*

So, you still feel me. Dive deep and fast.

No.

Don't trust anyone.

I'm coming back on that ship, Jocelyn pleaded.

You can't. Dive, Mli. Dive now.

Benlar was gone. She couldn't feel his emotions intertwining with hers. She swam faster, closing her eyes to shield them from the piercing water. Her hands hit an attacking shark.

CHAPTER 2

Aidan wiggled his hands, trying to free them from the rope that kept him tied to the walls of the storage room. Blood stained the white twine as his skin raked away with his determination to be free.

"Will you stop that?" Benlar yelled across the room, sitting on the floor.

Aidan glared at the man who had thrown the only woman he'd ever loved into the ocean to die. "Do not speak to me." Aidan twisted his hands again, trying to gain control.

Benlar rubbed his cheek against his shoulder, wiping drying blood from his face. A deep cut extended over his forehead into his hair. "Stop struggling. You're giving me a headache."

Aidan recoiled. "You threw her overboard!"

"Where she belongs."

"She was sick. Whatever she is, she will still die. Do you not see that?"

Benlar used his legs to push himself against the wall and stand. "Die from what? I saved her."

Aidan did the same and stood to his feet, facing his enemy. Both men, tied to opposite walls, leaned forward, stretching the fibers of the ropes digging into their skin.

"You killed her!" Aidan screamed.

"Then let me go, and I will save her again." Benlar lifted his chin.

Aidan leaned against the wall and struggled to reach into his jacket pocket. On the verge of dislocating his shoulder, Aidan wrapped his fingers around Benlar's medallion. He pulled out the coral trinket for Benlar to see. "Is this what you're asking for?"

Benlar smirked as he leaned against the wooden walls of the ship. "You know it's the only way."

"For you to escape?" Aidan dropped the trinket. It bounced then landed flat against his leather boot.

Benlar locked his eyes on the trinket. "You don't understand what she is. She needs me."

"She was fine until you boarded my ship."

"She will never be *fine* above water. This is her ocean. She has a responsibility to her kin," Benlar said.

Aidan shook the trinket from his boot. It clinked against the floor. "Who were you to her?"

Benlar slid back to the ground and closed his eyes. "We were lovers soon to be bound together." He opened his eyes, glaring at Aidan. "You see, Mr. Boyd, you were not the only creature in love with her."

Aidan's blood burned with hatred for Benlar. He shifted his eyes away from the merman. "Is she dead?"

"No."

"Will you protect her?"

"With my life."

"You had better." Aidan shifted his boot and kicked the trinket. It stopped inches away from Benlar.

Benlar stared at the medallion. "You'll never see her

again," Benlar said, looking up at Aidan. "She will never return to you."

Aidan met his stare. "We will see."

Benlar stretched his toe toward the coral medallion. The creak of the heavy door stopped him. Both men stared as Thomas walked into the room with a pistol in each hand.

He aimed the first one slowly at Benlar's head.

"What the hell are you doing, man?" Aidan demanded.

"He killed my beloved. And you"—Thomas aimed the second pistol at Aidan—"did too."

He pulled the trigger.

Aidan flinched, but nothing happened.

Thomas grinned. "I cannot have my captain murdered onboard. That would be bad for business. But a public hanging —that will be a sight to see."

"On what grounds?" Aidan asked, his eyes trained on the pistol still pointed at Benlar.

"Murder and mutiny, of course," Thomas answered.

"No one will believe you," Aidan snapped.

"Quite the contrary, sir. My fiancée rests at the bottom of the sea due to the quarrel between you and Mr. Benlar." Thomas took a step toward Benlar. "And you, Mr. Benlar."

He aimed the gun at his leg and fired.

The round bullet tore through Benlar's flesh and lodged against the bone. Screaming in pain, Benlar pushed down on the wound, trying to seal it. Blood seeped through his fingers, streaming onto the floor and toward the coral. Thomas picked up Benlar's only way home, pocketing his medallion.

"Scream all you like, Mr. Benlar. This is not the end."

Thomas walked out, leaving Aidan to watch Benlar bleed to death.

Its mouth stretched wide, parading rows of sharp teeth, the shark lunged. Jocelyn dove, swimming into deep waters with the shark chasing after her. The predator snapped his jaws at her tail. Her ears vibrated with the pounding of her heart.

A large formation of rocks altered Jocelyn's direction. She swayed her body to swim faster toward the safe haven, but the shark was faster. It bit the tip of her fin, pulling away a piece of skin. She screamed as blood misted into the blue water, dyeing it a dark purple.

Don't stop! Jocelyn yelled at herself, but the pain burned with each swipe of her tail, slowing her down.

The bloodthirsty shark quickened its speed, the savory taste still lingering on its tongue. It opened its mouth wide as it inhaled her bleeding fin.

She turned to see the shark's jaw closing. *No, no, no, no!*

An arrow shot through the water into the side of the shark. Veering left, the shark swam into the ocean away from its prey with a trail of blood following behind. Jocelyn continued to swim forward, still looking behind her. Another arrow pierced the giant fish. The giant shark paused for a moment, stunned, before retreating.

Jocelyn swam behind the rocks, hiding from the new threat. She wedged her body into a small cave, hopefully disappearing from view. *Don't find me. Please don't find me.*

I hear you. A woman's voice pushed its way into Jocelyn's mind.

Jocelyn squeezed her body against slimy algae on the rock wall as a mermaid, a crossbow strapped to her waist, swam past the opening. The mermaid's bright-red tail gliding through the water reminded her of the flame in the hearth of Edith's home in Ireland. The old lady had taken Jocelyn in when she washed to shore with no memory of who she was. Edith had named her Jocelyn and had taught her to adapt to the world above. Sadness caught in her throat.

Jocelyn watched her own blood thread its way out of the cave, giving away her location.

I'm not going to hurt you, the mermaid said. The creature swam into view, watching her. She raised her hands to show they were empty. *Come out.*

Who are you? Jocelyn asked.

I am Piean. We need to stop that bleeding before we both become shark bait.

Jocelyn could imagine this mermaid singing an enchanting song of lost souls with her silvery voice. *I'm not supposed to trust you.*

You have no choice. There's no one else here.

Piean won. Jocelyn put her hands on the edge of the rock and shoved into the open waters. She wrapped her arms around her naked chest.

Why are you unclothed? Piean asked.

Piean's torso was covered with seaweed woven into a skintight shirt with dark netting covering her gills, allowing the water to move freely in and out. A thin, raised layer of cinnamon-colored skin covered a glowing symbol on her chest —three circles overlapping each other, forming four triangles in the center.

Jocelyn brushed her thumb over the rough curve of the coral and smooth copper that was embedded, but not covered, by her skin. She was more exposed by the symbol than her naked body.

Embarrassed, she focused on Piean's weapon. The

crossbow fitted perfectly into a harness attached to two belts buckled around the mermaid's waist and thigh. The utility belt also held a satchel, a money purse, a blade, and a bag of arrows.

Piean opened the satchel and held out a spare shirt. *Here.*

Jocelyn reached out and took it. Piean turned as Jocelyn pulled the shirt over her head.

What happened to your clothes? Piean asked.

They burned away.

Piean spun around. *You were on the surface?*

Jocelyn nodded, pulling down the long sleeves of the dark-green seaweed shirt.

Piean swam close to Jocelyn. *I've never seen a shifter's mark before. What's it like up there?*

Jocelyn's fin tingled as she remembered sand pressing between her toes and the phantom smell of pine in the room she'd borrowed at Edith's. Here, the ocean tasted of salt and fear—but it was not like that before. When her family was one. Before the killing started. Her memories of both worlds were clear. She was not born a shifter, and her medallion would prove that, but she had stepped foot on land. Her grandmother had broken the laws. Jocelyn's heart skipped. Grandmother.

I need to get to Thessa.

Piean's gaze shifted from Jocelyn's hidden medallion to her eyes. *Do you know where you are?*

On land, she knew she was near Calcutta, India, but below, Jocelyn had no idea where she was. She remembered the city, her home, Thessa, but had never left its boundaries. She was lost.

How far am I? Jocelyn asked as a cloud of blood swirled around her from her bleeding fin.

Far, Piean answered.

Piean grabbed the blade from her belt, pressing her fingers to two copper rings. The blade glowed red as the water around it boiled.

Jocelyn stared at the mermaid.

You're still bleeding, Piean stated as she flipped upside down and pressed the flat side of the blade against Jocelyn's open wound.

Jocelyn screamed as her flesh burned with the touch of the knife. She smacked Piean with her tail.

Piean dropped the blade. *You stupid girl!* It landed with a thud, releasing a cloud of white sand and the heat it had held.

Camedia! You burned me!

Piean rolled her eyes. *Someone has been pampered. You're not bleeding anymore.*

We could have found a doctor.

Piean dove and grabbed her blade. *In the city, there are plenty of doctors, but out here we have to improvise.* Piean waved her knife, cooling it in the water before slipping it back into its case on her hip. *Do you have a name?*

Jocelyn stared at the small, red burn mark on her golden fin. The pain quickly dulled as she swatted it against the ocean. *Jocelyn.*

The name slipped from her mind as if it were really hers. Mli was her born name, given to her by her dead parents, but Jocelyn was who she longed to be again, the sorrow of her broken life hidden from her.

I can take you to Ommo. From there you have a two-week journey to the City.

Where is it?

Piean pointed north.

CHAPTER 3

"Has the bleeding stopped?" Aidan asked.

Eyes closed, Benlar shook his head no. A small trickle of blood dripped to the floor, reverberating in his ears.

"You have to stop it."

Benlar rolled his head to glare at Aidan. "I'm trying." He pressed on the wound, but blood continued to flow.

"You're going to bleed out."

"I thought that would make you happy."

Benlar shifted his weight, moving his leg. He bit back a scream as the open tissue rubbed together. Closing his eyes, trying to gain control, he envisioned Mli's blue eyes turning black with the sea, the first signs of morphing back into a mermaid.

The grinding of the heavy door's hinges stirred Benlar to open his eyes. A dark figure stood in the doorway. He took a step toward Aidan, a knife drawn. The blade slid through Aidan's ropes, releasing him. The person turned, leaving the shadows that concealed his identity. The small room melted away as the deep ocean filled Benlar's senses. His lungs gasped for air as the figure transformed into Mli. He reached out his untied hands.

He was a merman again, and he was home with her. He wrapped his hands around her face and kissed her. She kissed him back.

Mli pushed her body against his.

Mli.

Benlar lifted his head at the familiar voice. Avia, Mli's grandmother, drifted at the doorway, holding her hand out for Mli. Few merrows chose to age. The majority stayed young with frequent visits to hibernation chambers, where their bodies could rejuvenate and de-age. But Avia was different. She welcomed the effects of aging.

We have to go, Avia said as her white hair drifted around her. Her sad, wrinkled eyes stared at Mli. But there was more than sadness. Fear hid in the corner of her pale lips.

Mli cupped Benlar's face. *Find me when I am ready.*

Stay. I will protect you, he pleaded with the woman he loved.

Jocelyn swam her face inches from his. *This is going to hurt.*

Benlar peered into Mli's black eyes that reflected his image. *What?*

This is going to 'urt. Nicholas's voice bled out Mli's as the dream faded, leaving Benlar pinned down, screaming. "We 'ave to pull it out, Captain. It be rotting if we don't."

Aidan sat on Benlar's chest, holding him down. "Do what must be done," Aidan answered. "Give me your knife."

"Do you think it wise to be cutting him free?

"I'm not going to cut him free. We might need it if he turns on us," Aidan said.

Nicholas pulled a knife from his boot and handed it to his captain. "We could walk away, Captain. Let 'im die."

"No. He cannot die. Take the bullet out, Nicholas."

"Get off me!" Benlar yelled, the force of Aidan's body pressing his back against the wood floor, crushing his ribs.

"He be needing this." Nicholas shoved his belt into Benlar's mouth, pushing his tongue back. "Bite."

Benlar struggled to break free, but his strength gave way as Nicholas inserted his fingers into the wound and pulled the muscle apart.

Benlar's back arched as the pain numbed away the smell of his blood, his screams, and eventually the room, leaving him in darkness.

Jocelyn's muscles in her tail burned as she kicked to keep up with Piean.

How long were you above? Piean asked.

Months. I'm sorry, but I have to stop.

Jocelyn panted as her body stopped moving. They had been swimming for about an hour, and her transformation had drained her strength.

What's the matter?

Jocelyn lay back, drifting in the water. *I'm tired. Just give me a second.*

We're almost there. Ommo is behind the coral, Piean said, tapping her crossbow on her thigh.

A bright forest of pink, blue, and green coral branched up on the raised rocks, separating Jocelyn from the nearing civilization.

I don't believe you, Jocelyn answered, not moving. *You said that last time I asked.*

We should keep moving. These waters are not safe, especially since you are not armed.

Jocelyn stretched her spine. She swallowed the pain from

her weak muscles and queasy stomach. *I'm ready.* She kicked, moving forward. Piean rushed to take the lead again.

What were you up on land for? Piean asked, examining her.

To study, Jocelyn lied.

Something about Piean made Jocelyn not fully trust her. The shorter the answers Jocelyn gave, the more irritated Piean's voice became.

To study what? the young mermaid asked.

The weather, Jocelyn barked back. The endless questions were getting on her nerves. The time above was hers and hers alone. She had no desire to share it with a stranger. *Is Ommo a mining town?*

Piean nodded.

That's great, Jocelyn thought, blocking Piean from her deeper thoughts, a trick she'd learned from her grandfather.

Mining towns were dangerous because of the growing underground trade of illegal gases. Jocelyn glanced at Piean. She was warned never to trust anyone from the outskirts. Her stomach turned.

What type of mining? Jocelyn asked, watching Piean's weapons.

Natural gas. Piean stopped swimming, allowing Jocelyn to catch up. *There it is.*

Rock buildings erupted from the sand. Glass globe lampposts lined the structures, burning bright. Each one flickered with fire fueled from methane gas pumped from reservoirs under the seafloor. Glass domes around the flames held in oxygen, pumped from underground tubing, and kept out the ocean to allow the flame to burn.

Jocelyn blinked, her eyes sensitive to the light. Hundreds of watermills turned with the current, producing energy to illuminate the homes and businesses with electricity. The light glimmered in the water like small diamonds.

That's Ommo? Jocelyn asked.

The one and only, Mli.

Jocelyn's breathe caught in her chest.

Who's Mli? Jocelyn was bad at lying, and her voice cracked as she turned to look at Piean.

The crossbow was pointed at her heart, a burning arrow ready to strike.

I will pierce you and drag you back if you try to swim away. Piean's voice was strong and unyielding.

Why are you doing this?

They are looking for you, and there's a beautiful bounty on your head.

You're looking for payment…

No, I'm saving you, Piean said with a smile as she pushed against a coral wall, opening a doorway that led to an underground tunnel. She motioned with the tip of her arrow toward the entrance. *Get moving,* Piean ordered, looking over her shoulder.

The ocean began singing to Jocelyn in a whispered hush. The water swirled up her tail to the tip of her fingers as she gained control, but before she could command the sea, Piean hit her with the butt of her crossbow. The crack of her nose echoed in the water as a stream of blood drained out. The ocean calmed as Jocelyn bellowed in pain, unable to focus.

I said swim, Piean ordered. *Others are looking for you.*

Jocelyn swam through the doorway and under the settlement of Ommo, Piean not far behind.

CHAPTER 4

The swelling compressed the split bone in her nose, making everything hurt—even her teeth. Jocelyn's left hand held tight to her broken nose that was leaking blood behind her and Piean as they swam through the dark tunnel. Her eyes kept searching for light, but there was none to find. Jocelyn reached out her free hand, protecting her head from hitting what she could not see as she slowed down.

Keep moving, Piean ordered.

Where am I suppose to go? I can't see anything.

Straight.

Piean pressed the point of the arrow against Jocelyn's thigh. Anger festered under her skin as hair rose on the back of Jocelyn's neck. She inched forward into the darkness.

The walls of the tunnel closed in around them, and the water became warm and still. Jocelyn closed her eyes, trying to connect with the ocean. But it was quiet, leaving her to her own fight. Panic settled in Jocelyn's fast-beating heart. She had no weapon, no strength, no control over the ocean, and the bleak darkness bit at her soul, reminding her she was alone.

A blue glow flickered in her peripheral vision. Jocelyn turned her head to see Piean's hand pressed against the wall of the cavern. It was covered in small, bright-blue dots. The mermaid flung her hand forward as the blue gleam flickered alive, multiplying and encircling the tight tunnel in light.

Forgetting the pain from her nose and the threat of Piean's crossbow, Jocelyn marveled as her eyes adjusted to the brightness. The blue bioluminescent plankton fluttered with the movement of the mermaids' tails as they swam past and clung to their bodies.

Did you plant them here? Jocelyn asked.

No, not me.

Jocelyn looked back at the mermaid. Piean beamed as she floated in the light, unable to hide the amazement on her face. She was not much younger than Jocelyn, but her body was toned, ready to fight.

Piean's eyes met Jocelyn's, and her joy from the plankton quickly faded — replaced by animosity. This merwoman from the City was Piean's last hope of leaving Ommo and never coming back. She would just have to convince Laza, but that wouldn't be hard. He hated the Thessas as much as she did. She jabbed the tip of her arrow into Jocelyn's tail again.

Move, Piean demanded.

Damn you, Jocelyn yelled out as she pulled her fin away from the sharp point, glaring at Piean.

The bleeding stopped, Piean said with a grin. *I thought I was going to have to burn your nose.*

Jocelyn ran her fingers down her crooked nose, wincing with the sharp pain the touch brought to her face, but Piean was right. There was no blood in the water. Thank God. Jocelyn knew Piean wasn't joking about burning her face and sensed she might even enjoy doing it.

Where are you taking me? Jocelyn asked. The warm plankton tickled her skin as she swam through them.

To meet a friend.

Jocelyn's muscles screamed for her to stop, but she didn't want Piean to poke her again. She pushed forward, straining every bit of energy she had.

A round, silver door closed off the tunnel. A tree with thousands of leaves was carved into the metal, a star on its left side. Jocelyn stopped swimming, but her body twitched with movement. Piean kept aim at her as she pulled out a key from the purse attached to her belt. She unlocked the door, never taking her eyes off Jocelyn.

After you. Piean gestured with her head for Jocelyn to enter first.

A low copper glow illuminated a room. Jocelyn swallowed back her fear of what waited on the other side and swam in.

Nicholas dropped the crimson bullet to the ground, his fingers painted red with Benlar's blood. The old man wiped the sweat from his brow with his forearm—careful not to get any of the blood on his face. A lot of work still needed to be done.

Benlar's body slumped where he lay unconscious.

"He's still bleeding," Aidan stated, watching the red plasma seep out of Benlar onto the ground. Aidan could dance with a storm and not show any fear, but blood made his head spin. He licked his lips, trying not to be sick from the metallic smell.

Nicholas grabbed a rope and tied it around Benlar's upper thigh, cutting off the blood flow to his leg. The hemorrhaging continued.

Nicholas glanced up at Aidan. "If it don't stop, he'll die."

"Then how do we stop it?"

Nicholas shrugged, moving his shirt way from a hidden musket and a powder flask.

The wooden handle of the gun grabbed Aidan's attention. His mind spun. It was the only way to save him. He grabbed the powder flask.

"Wot you be doing?" Nicholas asked.

Aidan sprinkled the black gunpowder into Benlar's open wound, ignoring the urge to throw up. "Do you have a striker?"

Nicholas didn't question his captain. He handed him his flint and steel.

Aidan's eyes locked with Nicholas's. "Pray this works."

He squeezed the striker quickly, creating a spark that dropped onto the gunpowder. A small flame rose from Benlar's thigh, and the smell of burning flesh seeped into the air. The blood popped with the heat. Then the flame sizzled out, leaving blackened skin.

Aidan closed his eyes. His stomach flipped. He'd seen many men bleed, but never burned, and never at his hand.

Benlar flinched but didn't awaken.

"Clever," Nicholas said, examining the wound.

The hemorrhaging stopped.

Aidan moved off Benlar and rested against the cool wood of the belly of the swaying ship. He had saved Benlar, but Thomas was above waiting for a dead man, and it was only a matter of time until he achieved his goals.

CHAPTER 5

Water pushed against Jocelyn's body as the heavy door shut behind her, extinguishing the blue light of the algae that had surrounded her and Piean. A warm copper light flickered under a large glass dome in the center of a room shaped in a perfect sphere. Shadows darkened with the flicker of the encaged flame.

Jocelyn spun, her eyes widening. *What is this place?*

Corked jars and bottles lined tall shelves carved into the circular cavern. Severed fingers stacked on top of each other were in one jar. Flies flew in another, tapping against the glass. Algae cuffs hung from chains attached to holes in the wall. Jocelyn's reflection stared back at her in a large mirror covering part of the room. She counted three round, silver doors in the image. The one behind her led out, but the other two were unknown.

Jocelyn swallowed. The water tasted of iron and salt. She closed her eyes, trying to ignore the throbbing of her nose. But it didn't help. If she didn't get out of here soon, she feared her broken nose would only be the beginning of the pain she would endure.

Elder! Piean shouted behind Jocelyn.

Panic wrestled in Jocelyn's gut. This place was a cell used for torture, and she would never leave if this Laza entered the room.

Please. Whatever you want, my family can provide. Just let me go. Jocelyn's eyes locked with her captive's.

Piean shook her head. *Your family can't help me.* She raised her voice. *Laza, I have something you might want to take a look at. Where are you, old man?*

The silver door to the right of the mirror pushed forward. Terror pumped through Jocelyn's heart into her veins and into the water. A voice whispered to her, singing a sweet melody. The sea roared to life, ready to defend Jocelyn. A strong current slammed the door shut. Piean screamed as the water pinned her against the wall.

Turning, Jocelyn stared up at the trembling mermaid. *You should have let me go.*

Jocelyn pressed her hands forward, crushing Piean with the water. The young mermaid's screams echoed in Jocelyn's mind. With a flicker of her hand, Jocelyn could end Piean's life. She focused on the girl's neck. With a swift snap, she could break it without laying a finger on her.

The ocean slowly pushed Piean's head to the side.

Jocelyn relished the power warming her skin. She smiled at the petrified girl suspended above her. She could taste Piean's fear in the water, and it tasted sweet.

A metal ball spun faster and faster in the center of the room. The copper light burst into a bright flame and flickered with dancing gas. For a moment, Jocelyn could not see. She tried to blink away temporary blindness. Her eardrums shifted as the pressure in the room changed. Pipes at the bottom of the room opened, and water began to drain from the chamber.

Her fingers tingled as Jocelyn spun to see the mirror lit

and a man staring at her on the other side. He was standing on two legs. The control she had over the ocean slipped away, seeping through the cracks of the room. Once again, panic widened her eyes. She searched for a way out of the emptying fishbowl.

Piean slid down the wall into the remaining water. Her skin burned from the release of the ocean. Flipping, she dove to the bottom of the room and pushed her body against the ground. A click reverberated through the water as the ground shifted and a door opened.

The thud of the door shifted Jocelyn's gaze to Piean.

The trapdoor moved up from the ground with help from a metal spring, giving access to an underground room. Piean shoved into the darkness, scraping her scales against the sharp edges.

Jocelyn's head bobbed inches from the dropping surface of the water. Kicking with everything she had, she swam to escape with the girl. But she wasn't quick enough. The door shifted closed. Locking her in.

Water dripped from the walls as oxygen pumped in. Jocelyn's tail pressed against the bottom of the room. She tried to keep her head under the remaining water. The heat from the globe warmed her face like a kiss from the rising sun. It spun faster and faster, taking her ocean with it—draining out.

Her body slid against the cold ground as gravity pinned her down. Droplets from the ceiling fell from vents that pumped air into the room. The release of water slowed, allowing a foot of the sea to cover Jocelyn's body. She pressed her tail to her chest. Her exposed gills dried out with the lack of hydration, making it hard to breathe.

A voice boomed into the sphere. "That's better."

Why? she asked, turning her head to stare at the man.

"Use your mouth, dear. I hate mind-talk when I'm like this."

Jocelyn licked her lips before talking. "Why?"

The man laughed. "Because you would have killed my *sweet* Piean if I didn't do something. How, may I ask, were you doing that?"

"Fill up the tank, and I'll show you," Jocelyn said.

"No, thank you. I think we've had enough parlor tricks for one day."

The man pressed down on a lever. The globe spun faster, taking with it the last drops of water.

Jocelyn pressed her fingers into her medallion to pry it from her chest, to become human again, but it wouldn't budge. Her gills struggled to move as the air dried them out, and breathing became no more. She pushed the oxygen through her nose and mouth, trying to fill her lungs. But with her morphed body, her lungs were useless.

Darkness crept in.

"Sleep. I'll wake you soon," the man whispered.

Minutes faded away. Aidan watched Benlar's chest rise and fall, up and down, up and down, up and down. Ash and charred skin colored the bullet hole. A dark burgundy ring circled it. Aidan hoped the redness was from the trauma and not the beginnings of an infection. Benlar had to live for Jocelyn's sake.

Only a day had passed since Benlar had pressed Jocelyn's medallion into her chest. The coral and wiring had lit up and fused into her skin, becoming one with her body. Her weak, dying body. Closing his eyes, Aidan pictured her sinking to the bottom of the ocean. Her once-blue eyes, then yellow with death, searched for help. She was alone now. Aidan could not save her. Even if he dove into the abyss and swam deeper and deeper, he could not help her. He was human, and she was not. Aidan opened his eyes and stared at the motionless Benlar. But *he* could.

Aidan jumped to his feet and marched over to Benlar. He raised his hand and slapped the sleeping man across the face. Benlar didn't move, but he glared up at Aidan—his eyes raging dark green with swirls of black. Nicholas jumped to his feet, ready to fight.

"You need to go after her," Aidan said.

The darkness dissolved into the whiteness of his eyes as Benlar nodded. He shifted his gaze from the captain to Nicholas. "What is that old man doing here?"

"Be careful, Benlar. That old man saved your life." Aidan turned to Nicholas. "And you should return above before anyone comes looking for you."

"Why? Everyone knows I be down here with ye. Except dear Mr. Thomas Corwin. He, my captain, will be tasting the salt of the ocean soon."

A laugh escaped Aidan's lips. "I fear the sea might spit him back on the ship. And we can't risk the whole crew. If he drowns, there will be a hearing at court, and there are too many men to keep a secret."

"There already be one. He has turned the ship around. We be heading back to India, where he plans to turn you over to the authorities for mutiny."

"I figured. He is not a patient man," Aidan said.

"What about the medallion?" Benlar rustled as he shifted against the wall, dragging his body. A trail of drying blood followed his limp leg. "I need to return now."

Nicholas shook his head. Anger reddened his face. "She already be lost because of ye. She be down there alone, if not dead."

"She's not dead. You know that as well as I do. The ocean will not allow her to die," Benlar said.

Aidan's body ached from the tension he held in his shoulders. He rolled them, trying to loosen them, but relief did not come. "Your medallion is gone."

"The farther we move east, the farther we move from her. You need to find it." Benlar braced himself against the wall as he lifted himself up, favoring his wounded leg. His eyes watered from moving the injured leg, but he blinked it away.

"Ye shouldn't be walking on it," Nicholas spat out, still a little drowsy from not enough sleep.

"Can you return without it?" Aidan asked.

"No," Benlar said, grinding his teeth.

"Then what do you suggest?"

"I could throw ye in. See if ye could still swim," Nicholas said.

Retaining some balance, Benlar stepped forward, dragging his limp leg behind him. "Oh, I can swim, old man, and I can break your neck."

"I be having a strong neck." Nicholas stepped forward, ready to fight.

The ship rocked, shifting Benlar's footing. The bell of the boat echoed with his scream as his body slammed on the floor, tearing open the wound.

"Damn it!" Aidan rushed to Benlar's side.

He moved the leg to get a better look at the gash—blood seeped through the tear. It wasn't enough to bleed him out on its own, but Aidan was afraid with all the lost blood, Benlar might not be able to handle losing another drop.

Pulling off his left boot and stocking, Aidan wrapped the wool sock around the wound and pulled tight.

"Get me the damn medallion!" Benlar said through grinding teeth as the darkness invaded his eyes once more.

"Thomas has it."

"Then you know where to start." Benlar rested his head back and closing his eyes.

Aidan exhaled, then turned to Nicholas. "I believe it's still on him," Aidan said.

"I can 'ave a few men grab him."

Aidan shook his head. "That could turn sour quick. If there's a trial, I don't want anyone else accused."

Nicholas scratched his head, then his eyes brightened. "George!"

Aidan's eyebrows scrunched. "Who?"

"The cabin boy."

"What about him?"

"He can pickpocket anyone. Learned in the orphanage." Nicholas stood.

"That's great!"

"Go find the kid," Benlar said, his speech slurred.

Nicholas ignored the order and stared at Aidan, waiting. Giving a nod, Aidan approved the plan, and Nicholas was off to find the cabin boy.

"I hope they're quick," Benlar said. His eyes remained closed as blood seeped from the reopened wound.

Aidan swallowed back the urge to vomit. "We need to stop the bleeding again."

Benlar nodded.

Picking up the powder flask, Aidan sprinkled the black powder over Benlar's open lesion.

"Do you want something to bite down on?"

Benlar shook his head. "Just do it."

Aidan lit his match and ignited the gunpowder. Benlar howled as the scent of burned flesh filled the room once again. His erratic breathing heaved his chest in fast movements as time passed.

The sun moved past the porthole. Aidan and Benlar sat in silence, waiting for Nicholas to return.

Heavy, running footsteps pounded down the hallway toward their door. Aidan leaped to his feet and looked for a weapon. If it was Thomas with a gun, he wanted to be ready.

The door swung open before he could find one, and Nicholas ran in, closing it behind him. His breathing was labored.

"I got it!" the old man said, displaying his crooked teeth. "The lad be meant for a life of crime, snatching the medallion right from Mr. Corwin's pocket with his little finger."

Benlar fidgeted, his eyes wide with hope. "Where is it?"

Nicholas held up the emblem. Broken coral hung from the copper wire, distorting the swirl of Benlar's medallion.

Benlar shot up, ignoring the pain. "What happened to it?"

Nicholas shrugged.

"Thomas must've broken it," Aidan said.

Taking the trinket from the old man, Aidan placed it in his palm and walked over to Benlar and knelt down. The coral shifted in pieces, moving with the wiring. The once-perfect spiral sank inward, pressing against the small gears.

"It's shattered," Aidan said, holding it out to Benlar.

Benlar laced his fingers around the medallion, making sure not to touch Aidan, and lifted it. Panic rushed through his heart. If it worked, it would be a miracle. But it had to work.

Laying it on his chest, he waited for the warmth to sooth

his skin and mind, but the coral remained cold and unalive.

Aidan shifted to his knees, waiting, but the hopelessness in Benlar's eyes told him it wasn't going to happen. "Is that the only way?" Aidan asked. He pictured Jocelyn alone in the darkness.

Benlar nodded, unable to say the words.

Nicholas leaned over the two men, studying the trinket. "They're not touching the coral." He reached for the medallion.

"Don't touch me, human. It is your fault I'm still here."

"Bloody 'ell, man, do ye wish to stay with me or go back? I be done with ye and wish to throw ye back from where ye came." Nicholas grabbed the medallion with quick fingers. "Now let me see what can be done."

Aidan watched as the old man's weathered and callused fingers tightened around the coral ring, pressing them together. Gently, he slid the splintered pieces back into place. It appeared whole, but Aidan knew if Nicholas loosened his grip, the trinket would fall to pieces.

"Now ye try that."

Nicholas pressed the medallion to Benlar's chest.

The gears began to turn as the copper wiring burned bright orange. Benlar welcomed the familiar object back into his body as his skin grew around the spiral symbol. Small fragments of the blue coral shifted under the wire and into his skin.

"Ye shouldn't remove it again. I fear it won't last if ye do," Nicholas said.

"I'm done being human." Benlar tried to stand, but his leg buckled under him.

Aidan reached for his arm and pulled him to his side. Benlar was a good foot taller than he was, but he shrank with the pain.

"Are you going to be able to swim?" Aidan asked.

"Of course. I don't need legs in the water. Did the bleeding stop?"

Aidan pulled back the stocking. Blood covered the wound, making it hard to see if it was old or new. "I don't know."

"Let's hope it has. I need to get to the bow of the ship." Benlar hobbled toward the door.

"It's morning. It be shift change. The whole crew will be on deck," Nicholas said.

"I don't care. Get me to the water," Benlar ordered.

Aidan glanced over at Nicholas, and then at the door. Jocelyn was on the bottom of the ocean, waiting for her hero. He was going to send her one, even if it wasn't him.

CHAPTER 6

Her head rocked with the current in the room. Opening her eyes, Jocelyn stared at her golden tail, hanging inches above the rock floor. The cavern was submerged in water again. The ocean pulled at her motionless body, drifting her toward the surface, but the stainless steel chains and brown algae cuffs held her to the cavern wall. Her brain throbbed from the lack of oxygen that had brought her to unconsciousness many lost hours ago.

Jocelyn lifted her sore head. The ocean filled the room. Her arms, stretched from her sides, formed a cross on the gray wall. She wiggled her fingers and her tail to see if she had control of her body. Finding she did, Jocelyn pulled away from her shackles. But they held tight, only allowing her to space herself a few inches away from the wall.

The room was empty. The glow of the sphere in the center warmed the water that lapped over her. The ocean was quiet and held itself at a distance as she tried to gain control once more. Jocelyn ground her teeth, irritated by the fickle sea. There was no power left in her. No connection to help her escape. She was alone. Her only hope was the very people who imprisoned her.

Hello, Jocelyn yelled out into the room.

She shifted as the quietness settled into her bones, and her lips quivered. On land, tears would line her face, but here the ocean absorbed them, claiming one more piece of her.

Hello, she whimpered.

Oh. That's enough of that.

The door to the left of the mirror slid open as the man who'd been standing on two legs swam in. His graying red hair swayed with the moving water. He kicked his white tail to move closer to Jocelyn. He wore a leather vest with many bulging pockets.

Please. Just let me go. Please, Jocelyn pleaded.

Hold on. You, missy, almost killed my sweet Piean. Why would I just let you go?

His black eyes examined her as if assessing the risk of drawing even closer. He kicked his fin as he pulled a syringe from a pocket and slipped the metal cover off the long needle. The glass barrel of the syringe was empty. He slipped two fingers into two of the rings and his thumb on the plunger.

I am a bit curious how you do what you do, Mli.

The merman's voice emitted her name with ease, as if singing it to her for the hundredth time. Jocelyn's brow furrowed as she examined his face, filtering through her past.

On Aidan's ship, her memories had washed in, lifting the shadows of her forgotten life. But this merman was a dark figure with no face and no name.

What are you going to do?

Jocelyn's fingers curved around the rusted chains. If there was a weak spot, she would find it.

Don't fret. It won't hurt a bit.

The merman grabbed her arm and drew her closer to him. In a flash, he tied a rubber bull kelp around her forearm and snap it against her skin. His fingers tickled the crease of her arm as he ran them over her skin. He felt for her veins. Jocelyn tried to yank her arm from him, but his grip held tight, bruising her skin.

Don't be a child. Hold still. He injected the sharp needle into a swollen blood vessel.

Jocelyn's breath sputtered from the sharp pain, but it was quickly replaced with curiosity. She watched her blood fill the glass container of the syringe. *Are you a doctor?*

The merman's lips twitched. *Of sorts. Are you a mage?*

Jocelyn glared at him.

Are you? the merman asked.

She shook her head no. Her eyes burned.

The merman smirked. *Don't be so serious.*

He retracted the needle from her arm and applied pressure over the puncture. *Did your grandfather tell you of the mage and the fish?*

How do you know me? How do you know my Grandfather?

He pushed away her arm and inserted the end of the needle into its metal cover, twisting it tight to keep any more water from contaminating the sample.

I worked for him.

Jocelyn's stomach dropped. *You worked with my grandfather?*

Yes. Well, I worked under him. Helo was a good merman, but he liked his privacy. He would give enough information to keep them happy, then keep the rest for himself. Very smart merman, your grandfather. And you. Everyone knows who you are.

The merman's fading red hair fluttered around his face as he placed the syringe into his vest pocket. He grabbed Jocelyn's face and tilted her head back, examining her nose.

Jocelyn's muscles tightened, but she didn't struggle. There was no way out.

Your nose is broken.

I know. Your sweet Piean did it.

That one has a temper. But she is very good at her job.

Jocelyn locked eyes with the merman. *How do you know me?*

I met you when you were a little one, but the world knows you because you are wanted in Thessa.

Jocelyn's heart pounded in her chest, and she licked her lips, tasting the salt of the ocean. Being wanted by the city was an unsaid death sentence. *I want to go home.*

I know, dear. But first we need to set that nose.

The tenderness in the merman's voice allowed Jocelyn's lips to pull back into a smile. She swatted her tail to appear tall. The merman's kindness faded with the echo of the chains.

What do you want with me?

The merman beamed at her. *I thought you would never ask. I want to know why the Descendants fear you. Now hold still. This is going to hurt.*

The merman squeezed his thumbs against the bridge of her bent nose and pushed the bone back into place.

Jocelyn screamed, releasing a giant air bubble that floated toward the ceiling.

Benlar's limp leg dangled behind him as Aidan and Nicholas held him up. The rocking of the ship demanded the men balance themselves against the passageway walls. The cool, salty ocean misted the entrance to the ship's deck, carried by a gust of warm air. Benlar inhaled his world. Once he leaped into the ocean, the pain would wash away, leaving him in his true body. His right body. Not this flawed vessel that broke too easily.

Nicholas climbed up the steep stairs first and poked his head out to survey the situation.

"There be a large bunch of men, but no Mr. Corwin," Nicholas whispered.

"That will have to do," Aidan said. Blood pooled around the men's shoes. "Are you sure you can do this? I fear you might be losing too much blood."

Benlar huffed. "Get me to the ocean. If I am to die, it will not be on land."

"I'm not asking for your sake. I'm asking for hers."

"Get me to the sea," Benlar said. This man loved his Mli. This unworthy human was risking everything he had to save her. To give her a chance, even if it was without him. Benlar grabbed the rail, ready to hoist up his good leg one step at a time. "She can't return to you. You know that?" Benlar said over his shoulder.

Aidan's stomach turned with the smell of blood, and his heart broke. "I pray you are wrong."

"You only love her because she tricked you into believing it was real. She is a creature of the sea, a goddess above your kind. The way she talks, smells, breathes. We are superior. An exotic rush of forbidden power, that's all *she* is. And she lured you in with her scent."

The memory of Jocelyn's sweet perfume kissed Aidan's nose.

"You have no idea what is real and not. I love her. I will always love her," Aidan said as he stepped out of the blood.

"I'm telling you this because she will realize what she did and know it wasn't true. She fooled you. That's what we do. That's how we hide in your world and examine your kind. She will never return, because you never truly loved her."

Benlar pushed up the stairs, leaving Aidan in his shadow. A rush of guilt weighed him down, but Aidan deserved to know. A creature from the sea could never love a landwalker. Mli was no different.

Aidan's hands trembled and his mind spun as he questioned his own heart. He knew the lore of mermaids bringing men to their deaths with their beauty and songs. If they were true, then Benlar was speaking truth. Aidan grabbed the rail. In Ireland, he had questioned his own sanity, falling for her after only a few meetings. On the ship, their secret affair was bound together with his desire to be with her. With her gone and him left alone, the lust was gone, but his heart ached as if he'd lost part of himself. He could be a blind man, and without a word spoken, see her enter the room. He longed for that Jocelyn. The one who warmed his soul in the darkness.

Benlar limped onto the deck, stumbling to keep his footing.

Aidan emerged out of the doorway and stepped up to Benlar. He wrapped Benlar's arm around his waist, becoming his support.

Benlar turned and stared at him as the sailors noticed the two men.

"If it wasn't real, then why can I still feel her?" Aidan led Benlar toward the rail of the ship. Water sprayed from waves onto the wooden planks.

The green of Benlar's eyes disappeared as his pupil opened wide and turned black. His transformation had begun. "That's the problem with being with her. She leaves a wound that never heals without her touch."

Aidan struggled to breathe, watching this creature change in front of him. He grabbed the wet rail as sailors circled them. Nicholas rushed to keep the crowd at bay.

"Keep yer distance men. Let the captain to his job."

The men watched as Aidan stared into the ocean.

Benlar rested both hands on the rail, trying to get over the boat's edge. But his strength was gone, left in puddles.

"I know you love her. But she doesn't love you," Aidan said.

Benlar turned to Aidan. "She will never return."

Aidan shook his head. "We'll see." He grabbed Benlar's back and shoved him over the rail.

A wave crashed against the ship, swallowing Benlar as he hit the water.

The sailors rushed to the side of the ship. Each one peered into the water, searching for Benlar as Aidan pushed through the crowd. He knew Benlar would never surface. The sea had its child back.

Aidan exhaled. His world of facts and certainties had crumbled. His life of right and wrongs, blurring together. Creatures of fiction had appeared before him, leaving a bad aftertaste. He began to question everything. If he really was in love with Jocelyn, then he had sent his biggest threat to save her. Another man who would die for her. Aidan was left alone in a world where he had never belonged, other than on the ocean.

Aidan descended the stairs to the belly of the ship. Anger festered under his skin. He was done doing what was right. He marched toward Thomas's quarters, ready to take back his ship.

CHAPTER 7

Aidan didn't allow himself to think. He slammed his fist on the heavy wood door at the end of the hallway. Footsteps drummed across the concealed room. Aidan pounded again.

Thomas swung open the door, holding tight to a pistol. "What the bloody hell are you...?"

Aidan collided against Thomas, sending his ex-employer to the ground.

Wide-eyed, Thomas struggled to his feet. The room reeked of brandy. Aidan shoved him down before he could get his balance.

Thomas slumped to his elbows, tired and drunk. "I see you win in popularity," Thomas slurred, waving the pistol toward Aidan.

Aidan slapped the gun out of Thomas's hand and grabbed him by the shirt.

"Do you know what you are doing?" With every word, Thomas released a toxic level of alcohol from his breath.

Aidan ignored the urge to turn away from the man's breath. "I have an idea."

He lifted Thomas to his feet, holding him upright long enough for him to gain his balance. Thomas smoothed the wrinkles from his shirt.

"If I am hurt or killed, there will be a hearing, and...and justice will be served. Not just to you, but the whole crew," he said, followed by a hiccup.

"I'm not here to kill you." Aidan walked over to the open bottle of brandy on the desk and poured himself a glass. "I'm here to make a deal."

"A deal!" Thomas spat out. "You are in no place to make such a request."

"You are in no place to deny me." Aidan took a sip. The back of his throat burned as the warm liquid slid down. "Accidents happen on the sea all the time. There is a crew of very loyal men..."

"I understand." Thomas sauntered over to the bottle and reached for it. Aidan grabbed it before his employer could seize it.

"You've had enough," Aidan said, taking another drink.

"I could argue that."

Thomas's room was as large as the captain's quarters, with a desk and a full bed. When the ship was built, Thomas's father made sure to have a spare room incorporated for his visits aboard. This way there was no disruption of living spaces on long voyages.

Thomas sat on at the edge of his messy bed. "What do you want?" Thomas asked, brushing his hand through his sandy blond hair.

"I want my ship back."

Thomas smiled at the request. "You are to be charged with mutiny. I'm not going to give you *my* ship."

Aidan grabbed the chair from the desk, turned it to face Thomas, and sat. Locking eyes with Thomas, he took another drink.

The dull silence crowded the small space, making it unbearable.

Thomas exhaled. "The men hate me. I know this. But, my dear man, who will protect you when they are kept from their wages and employment? If I am harmed or murdered, what do you believe will happen to this company? No one will hire a crew who lost their employer, no matter how accidental it was."

Thomas reached for the bottle again, and this time, Aidan allowed him to take it.

"You are not their hero, but their destroyer." Thomas pressed the glass to his mouth and drank the brandy.

Aidan leaned back in his chair, twirling the small glass in his fingers. "You don't understand, Mr. Corwin. The deal I am making is not to stay in your employment. In fact, I'm purposing that this ship be retired from your father's establishment…"

"*My* establishment!"

Aidan grinned. "Your *father's* establishment before any dramatic situations should occur."

Thomas hugged the bottle. "How dare you threaten me."

"You're drunk. I'll allow you to ponder my arrangement."

Aidan stood and drank the last of the liquor in his glass. He placed the glass on the desk and peered out the porthole. The morning sun reflected off the calm waters in bright crystals. His heart thudded in his chest, but he maintained his breathing.

He had thrown away his livelihood in one rash moment, but excitement masked his fear. He smiled at the rolling waves. Freedom from society's rules blanketed him in a wave of courage.

"You speak of piracy," Thomas said.

Aidan turned to face the proud man. "If it must come to that."

"And the men? Do you damn them to a life of crime because of your selfish heart?"

Aidan's heart dropped. His mind was so locked on his own desires, ridding himself of Thomas's pounding fist, that he had not thought of the dangers he might put his crew in.

Thomas snickered. "You, my friend, could never be a pirate. You care too much." He took another swig. "Be a chap and close the door when you leave." Thomas lay back on his feather mattress.

Rage seeped through Aidan's body and mind. Losing control, he grabbed the pistol from the ground and marched over to Thomas.

Before Thomas could sit up, Aidan smacked the butt of the gun across the man's face. A loud thud of metal crashing into bone filled the room as the gun ripped open Thomas's cheek.

Aidan pressed the barrel of the gun to Thomas's temple. Brandy spilled from the open bottle, staining the white covers purple. Tears of sweat clustered on Thomas's forehead.

"I am not your friend. I am not your captain. And *you* are a dead man if you mock me again," Aidan said.

Thomas nodded, the drunkenness quickly fading.

Aidan stepped away. "Clean up. I expect your full corporation by noon." Aidan turned to leave. "Also, don't leave this room. I've already thrown one man overboard, and I find I quite liked it."

Aidan slipped the pistol into his belt and slammed the door behind him.

The water rushed into Benlar's lungs as he inhaled the salty ocean. The transformation ignited under his skin, melting away his human clothes. His medallion burned brightly. Closing his eyes, Benlar went limp.

The sea held and rocked him as his body tore itself apart. Gills ripped through his chest. His fingers webbed. Dark-silver scales sliced through his legs and covered his wound. But he was numb to the metamorphosis.

Benlar was his true self in mere minutes. His inner flame dimmed as he opened his black eyes. He was in his world. Now he had to go home.

He kicked his tail hard to propel himself forward, but he flinched from the intense pain in his thigh and rubbed where the bullet had entered his leg. He ground his teeth from the deep throbbing of the damaged tissue.

The change only covered the wound, but the internal damage was still there, and it hurt.

Benlar kicked again. He had to move. Pain pulsated through his body, but he blocked it. He couldn't rest in open waters — too many dangerous factors.

If he could reach the city of Ommo, he could mend there. Ommo was the largest dwelling for miles in these waters, and the first place to start searching for Mli.

Benlar focused on Mli's face as he swam east toward the mining town.

The doctor inserted strips of cloth into Jocelyn's nostril. Blood ran down the back of her throat. The iron taste reminded her of undercooked meat. Nauseated, Jocelyn coughed up the blood and spit it out, staining the water.

Don't do that. The merman waved at the floating particles. *I don't wish to breathe in your bodily fluids,* the merman said. He handed her a towel then pulled on the chains. A click rattled through the water as the heavy restraints extended from within the wall, dropping Jocelyn's hands to her side. *Spit into this.*

Jocelyn shook the chains. *You could just release me.*

Not yet. I would like to have a conversation with you first.

Jocelyn stretched her cuffed hand to her mouth and coughed into the towel. *You already know who I am. I'm assuming you're Laza?*

I am. Laza swam over to a shelf and pulled out a glass jar.

What type of conversation would you like to have? I'm quite good at small talk.

Mli, I'm not interested in getting acquainted. I would like to know what you are capable of. Laza turned and held out a jar filled with pebbles. *Don't let it break.*

He dropped the heavy container.

Jocelyn rolled her eyes as the heavy jar sank to the hard ground. *It doesn't work that way.*

How do you believe it works, then? Laza asked, turning to grab something else from the built-in shelves.

A light flickered on and lit up the room on the other side of the mirror, taking away the reflection. Piean glared at Jocelyn through the thick glass. Laza beamed at the mermaid and waved. Piean continued to scowl.

She doesn't understand what you are, Laza said.

And you do? Jocelyn asked.

I have an inkling. Now, dear, how do you think your power works? I don't know. It just happens.

Laza toyed with a blade before setting it down and lifting a short spear. He rolled his fingers over the handle. *How do you feel when it happens?*

Jocelyn stared at the weapon. She knew he wanted answers, but she was curious how far he would go to get the reaction he was looking for.

Do you feel fear?

Jocelyn nodded.

Threatened.

Do you mind putting that away?

Laza held up the spear. *Does this make you nervous?*

Of course. I'd be a fool if it didn't. She was done being picked on.

He pointed the tip toward her. *Did your grandfather tell you the tale of the mage and the fish?*

You've already asked that.

You haven't given me an answer.

Jocelyn's grandfather, Helo, was a quiet merman with a contagious smile. She remembered his hand engulfing hers in a protective embrace as they swam through the reef forest. He called her *the little light.* He was a smart merman. He knew every species of plant and animal her little fingers pointed out. He had worked for Thessa, but he never spoke of his job. Instead, he told her fairytales.

Jocelyn nodded at Laza then spoke. *A mage came from an in-between world, a place where magic fuels its existence and life never changes. Where mermaids are born with tails, not legs. She left her world, with a vial of tears from a dying mermaid, and came to the land above. Blending in with the humans, she hoped to grow her powers and then return to her home to rule. But unlike her land, magic was different and rare. When she did learn to master a small portion of the magic, she was discovered and hunted by the humans. The mage took to the sea. She collected scales and made a dress of them. On the first full moon of autumn, she put on the dress, walked into the ocean, and drank the mermaid tears, becoming the first mermaid in our ocean.*

Laza's eyes glinted like a young child hearing his favorite bedtime story, but he stayed silent, letting her continue.

I know this is a simple version of our origin story, but... Her voice trailed off.

The elders created us with their technology, just as the mage created the dress. Do you know how the story ends? he asked.

Jocelyn cleared her throat again. Less blood rolled over her tongue. *It's just a fairytale.*

How does it end? Laza asked.

The mage has a child of the ocean, Piean said.

Jocelyn's eyes widened. Her grandfather had told her this version many times. A child made in another world and brought to ours. This ending was only told by him, and he would whisper it when he retold the tale. Her grandfather knew Laza and had trusted him with this.

What does it have to do with her? Piean asked, pointing at Jocelyn.

Laza beamed at both girls. *Not created, but born of the ocean.* He took the end of the spear and swam over to Jocelyn. *I would like to try something, if you don't mind.*

Jocelyn shook her head. *I do mind.*

Then you do it, he said, putting the small spear in her hand. *I imagine you want answers as much as I do.*

He swam away from her and stopped next to Piean.

And what am I suppose to do? Jocelyn asked, her heart racing.

Remove your medallion, Laza answered.

Piean's body shifted. *She can't turn human underwater. She'll drown.*

Laza grinned at Jocelyn. *Not if she's the mage's child.*

This merman was mad, but Jocelyn was curious. The

ocean was its own master, but she couldn't deny she had control over it. It breathed with her. It was her shelter and protector.

She ran the blade of the spear under the raised medallion, separating it from her skin. The gears under the coral family symbol sputtered before stopping. Jocelyn clutched the trinket and ripped it away from her chest, waiting for the transformation to kill her.

Piean swam closer, wide-eyed. *That can't be.*

Laza took her hand. *My dear, she's who I've been searching for.*

Jocelyn dropped the medallion, allowing it to flutter with the ocean current to the ground. She kicked her tail and lifted her head high. The ocean sang to her, claiming her as its own. She was the only true mermaid.

CHAPTER 8

The suffocating embrace of the ocean slithered under Jocelyn's fingernails, up her hand, and into her spine. The hair on her neck stood, tickling her. This was not right. It shouldn't be possible. She glanced at the medallion on the sea floor.

She'd spent her whole life attached to the trinket. It was her life source, power, and history, but now it was nothing more than jewelry. Panic crept over her. Everything she'd been taught was wrong. Everything she believed about her past, people, and history was wrong. She was living proof.

If she was different, then *she* was a threat to Thessa and the Descendants.

Her uncontrolled heartbeat stuttered. Her parents died because of what she was. The cold algae cuffs pressed into her wrists as she sank down.

Frozen, Piean stared at Jocelyn, unable to process what she'd witnessed. The girl was still a mermaid. Breathing in the ocean with no difficulties. Piean ran her fingers over her medallion infused under her skin. The chill in the water bit at her fin.

As a child, she had been warned never to remove her family mark. It was the family crest that identified one's origins

—one's placement in this world under the rule of the Descendants.

The eight Descendants were the first to call the ocean their home. They were the oldest and strongest creatures underwater. Having discovered the *turritopsis rubra*, the Descendants harnessed the jellyfish's ability to de-age.

And with false promises, they created a system of obedient followers, each fighting to receive the gift of prolonged youth. The strongest were chosen for tasks deemed worthy of exploration. After generations, these bloodlines were bestowed eternal life.

Piean's symbol was marked for the unwanted, the throwaways. Destined to die in a mine or servitude. Unworthy of the gifts from the city.

Piean licked her lips, tasting the salt from the sea. *What are you?* she asked.

Jocelyn stared at the medallion, unable to move. *I don't know.*

You have to know something, Piean persisted.

Laza picked the medallion off the ground and put it into his vest. *Leave the poor girl alone,* Laza said, pulling a key from a pocket.

Do you not see what I see? Piean pointed at Jocelyn.

Laza smiled. *Of course, but can't you also see she knows nothing?*

Piean shook her head, clenching her jaw. To argue with the old merman was useless.

Laza unlocked the cuffs on Jocelyn's wrist.

Sinking, Jocelyn's tail hit the floor. She leaned back, resting her head on the wall. Rough rocks snagged her auburn hair as she turned to look at Laza, who sat beside her.

The wrinkles around his milky blue eyes folded inward as he smiled at her. Jocelyn couldn't help but wonder how old he really was.

I would like to go home, Jocelyn said, playing with the webbed skin between her fingers.

You can't, Laza said.

Anger festered and burned the tips of her ears. *I want to go home now.*

The old merman stared at her. *You have no home.*

I know that!

The familiar voice of the ocean whispered to her as the water between Jocelyn and Laza thickened, pushing them apart. The doctor kept his eyes on hers. *Tell me what you're feeling,* he ordered.

Her heart raced as she focused on flutters of panic beating in her chest. Her cheeks heated, and deep in the back of her mind, the voice spoke. It sang to her as it did on land. A gentle voice breathed life into her.

Do you hear it? Jocelyn asked. *It wants me to remember.*

What does it want you to remember? Laza asked.

It won't tell me, Jocelyn replied.

The emotions rising in her subsided as the world slowed to a soft pulse. The voice called both of Jocelyn's names, without prejudice to the land or sea.

What do you hear, child? Laza leaned closer to her, but the ocean shoved him away.

The clear water darkened around Jocelyn.

What is happening? Piean cried as she backed toward the wall and the door.

Shh! Laza said, locking his eyes on Jocelyn. *Piean, go into the glass room.*

Piean didn't need to be told twice. She darted for the door, swam through, and bolted it. She kicked to the control panel and window that peered into the sphere room, where Jocelyn and Laza remained.

What do you want me to do? she asked, directing her thoughts only to Laza.

Her fingers danced over knobs, buttons, and levers. This was Laza's contraption, and Piean was untrained in how it functioned, other than a few over-the-shoulder glances when he was working.

If need be, pull the copper lever to your right, Laza ordered.

The water surrounding Jocelyn tinted darker as Piean grabbed the handle of the thick metal lever of the draining system. The pressure of her touch moved the lever down. Air bubbles rose from the ground vents as fans turned below the ground.

Not now! Laza screamed.

Piean's hand shot away from the control panel. *Sorry.*

The bubbles fluttered up toward the ceiling, pressing around Laza and Jocelyn. Holding out her hand, Jocelyn froze the air pockets in the water.

Laza couldn't help but clap. *So you do have control?*

Do you hear it? Jocelyn asked again.

She thought she heard Laza say no, but it was unclear as the distant voice drowned out his, invading her mind. It called itself Keto. The darkness grew, concealing Jocelyn in blackness. Energy prickled the hair on her arms. Was she in control or the ocean?

Now! Laza yelled.

Piean pulled the lever as the blackness shot out and the spherical room turned black, consuming Laza and Jocelyn in its wake.

The waters became harder to breathe as Benlar entered Ommo. The swim was shorter than he thought, and he was thankful Aidan's ship hadn't sailed too far from the town. The seaweed that grew around the town flicked with the rough current of the busy town and the ocean's unpredictable shifts. Ommo was the leading supplier of methane clathrate — methane gas trapped in ice-like crystal. Easy to transport and carry, it was exceedingly valuable. It provided jobs for most of the occupants of the town. If it ceased to run, then Ommo would decay to nothing more than a ghost town.

Merpeople looked toward the surface, but the water was calm above. If there was a storm, it wasn't from the sky.

Benlar's tail ached with each kick, but he blocked the pain. The tavern was in the heart of the town. He could see the tall building's slate roof covered in barnacles, peering above the other businesses that lined the long street.

He swam faster. His reflection bounced off the shop windows.

A rogue current rammed into him, pinning him to a brick building for a moment before changing directions. The water was different. Dangerous.

Parents grabbed their playing children and rushed them inside as other merpeople held on to lampposts, trying to get a glimpse of the source of the underwater storm.

Maybe a mine is in trouble, Benlar thought.

Ommo was one of the best mining towns in the Indian Ocean, but accidents did happen. Except this wasn't like a mine explosion or the occasional earthquake.

Benlar kicked forward, but the ocean shoved creatures around with an invisible hand, as if it were alive.

The sign of *Mr. Margo's Tavern and Rooms* swung with the

rough current. Small sand twisters pelted the closed door as they spun by.

Benlar thrust open the door. Merrows huddled around the stone-framed window, peering at the underwater storm. The barkeep was the only one who glanced his way.

Have you heard anything about this? The overweight merman pointed outside. His blue seaweed shirt hugged a little too tight.

Benlar shook his head no. *Was there an explosion at the mine?*

This is no explosion, the barkeep said, rubbing his hand over his bald head.

Benlar took a seat at the bar. The tall chairs allowed his tail to rest without touching the rock floor.

I need the key to my room, Benlar said.

You might want to wait it out down here first, the barkeep said, watching the window.

I'll be fine.

The barkeep shrugged. He reached for a board, with numbers one through twenty painted on it, where thin keys dangled below the numbers. He grabbed key nineteen.

You're paid up for the rest of this week.

Good. Thank you, Benlar said, rubbing his tail.

The merman handed him the key. *Please let me know if you hear anything. This weird behavior is not good for the town. There will be questions, and the more answers I have, the better for business.*

Benlar nodded. He liked the barkeep, even though he didn't know his name. The merman didn't ask questions when he requested to leave his key at the desk for a few days, then left without a shirt or supplies. And now, the merman still didn't ask anything when Benlar came back, four days later.

He shifted out of the chair and swam up a stair-less case to the second floor. The stone building swayed with the push and pull of the current.

On the third floor, the building swayed.

Benlar guided the key into the door of room nineteen and turned. The door opened with ease. As requested, the room was untouched, as it was the day he left. His clothes hung over his bag on the bed. His blades and crossbow were on the metal desk. Swimming to the other side of the room, he ran his fingers under the desk. A pouch dangled from a string tied to the bar holding the furniture together.

Splitting his life savings in half, he'd left a money bag in his room and had taken one on land—which Thomas had taken for passage on his ship. Benlar untied the bag from its hiding place and peered in. Pearls and small gold coins adjusted with the movement. When he'd left the tavern in search of Mli, he figured he would come back to an empty room. He was relieved to see it wasn't so.

Lying down, he kicked the bag and clothes off. They descended to the floor, the water moving the loose articles around the small room.

Benlar closed his eyes. From morphing to the pain in his tail, he was exhausted. Sleep overcame him, blocking out the raging ocean.

Aidan submerged his hands in the washbasin. He scrubbed until the lavender soap foamed over the hair on his arms and the dried blood faded into the cool water.

Gregory paced the captain's quarters. Worry lines indented the first mate's forehead. He fiddled with the fray of his stained shirt. "What can be done?" Gregory asked.

"I have made a choice that affects the crew. I need to address them. I will not force this on any of you." Aidan dried his hands on a cotton towel.

Jocelyn's sweet perfume lingered in the placid air. This room was full of unwanted reminders. A two-sided comb rested near the washbowl. Aidan ran his calloused fingers over the fragile teeth and pulled a strand of hair from the comb. He rolled it between his fingertips. He questioned his own sanity when he was with her. The secret embraces and stolen kisses — were they nothing more than her bewitching him? Or was it more?

He dropped the loose hair to the floor. The only way to find out if she loved him was to see her again. The ocean was the only way to stay connected with her. He had to convince the crew to follow him into the unknown, or abandon them and find a new one in India. Either way, *he* would not leave the ship or the sea.

"I don't think this a wise choice of action, Captain," Gregory said. "If we resupply in India then travel back to England, there will be enough time to regain Mr. Corwin's trust in your ability to man his ship. He is a reasonable man."

"Are we speaking of the same man?" Aidan asked, pulling the blood-covered shirt over his head.

"You have a crew who will stand behind you, sir. We will all testify…"

"Do you truly believe there would be a trial?" Aidan opened the porthole and poured the red water from the washbowl into the ocean.

Gregory stopped pacing. "He would have to."

"He is a businessman. A trial would be bad for business. It will never come to that. I cannot and will not return."

Aidan poured the remaining clear water from a pitcher into

the bowl and cleaned his chest. He patted himself dry with a rag. The cool water was refreshing in the sweltering humidity. In long strides, Aidan made his way to the closet in hopes of finding a clean shirt. The ship's mild rocking was broken by a choppy patter of waves hitting.

Gregory sat on a wooden chair as small objects rolled on the desk behind him, catching on the lifted edges. He wiped his brow with the back of his hand. "I fear you will regret this decision."

Aidan opened the doors of the closet and peered at the solitary leather jacket in the armoire. The same jacket he had covered her with on the day they'd met in Ireland. He had dragged her from the freezing water, believing she was attempting to end her life. He knew the truth now. She was only trying to go home. If he would've known what she was from the beginning, would he have fallen for her, or would he have allowed the ocean to take her?

He ran his hand down the arm of the coat. If it was a trick of false love, then why had she kept this? Dropping the heavy fabric, he watched it sway for a brief moment.

"It is the only decision I can make. Gather the crew. I need to speak with them." Aidan closed the doors of the closet, leaving the coat.

CHAPTER 9

Aidan's lips brushed Jocelyn's. His fingers danced up her spine to the nape of her neck, playing with her hair. His body pressed to hers. She pulled away. His smiling eyes beamed at her. He'd found her.

Jocelyn reached to grab his hand but instead found a heavy seaweed blanket weighing her against the soft mattress, preventing her from drifting up.

Good. You're awake. How do you feel? Laza asked.

Jocelyn sat up and scooted into the corner, where the bed met the wall. The room was crowded with shelves full of books, and metal chests littered the floor. A mosaic of barnacles covered the clutter, indicating this storage room was not used often. A gas wall lamp lit the room, its flame covered in a glass dome.

I don't know. A dull thud pulsated in her head. *What happened?*

Laza sat on the edge of the bed frame. He grabbed a sealed glass jar, a thin straw protruding from the lid, from a side table and handed it to Jocelyn. A dark-brown liquid swirled within.

She took the rubber straw and bit it with her teeth, separating the folds of the top that blocked the drink from escaping into the ocean. The bitter flavor glided over her tongue, making her wince. She wished she could smell the coffee as she had in Henry's galley on Aidan's ship.

She wasn't thirsty, but she welcomed the change over salt water and the much-needed caffeine boost.

Well, my dear, you almost destroyed Ommo.

Gagging on the coffee, Jocelyn dropped the jar. It drifted to her lap.

Don't worry, you didn't succeed. My lab is in disarray, but it's nothing we can't fix. I must say, it was rather remarkable. Laza kicked off the bed and swam to the door.

I don't know what happened. It was as if someone else was in the room with us. Someone in my head.

We are all in each others' heads.

Jocelyn picked up the jar and set it on the table. *This was not mind-talk. It was different. Deeper.*

Do you think you can do it again?

Do you think it is wise? I don't have control, Jocelyn said, kicking the suffocating blanket off.

You need to learn how to control it.

I don't think I can.

You haven't tried. You've allowed your muddled emotions to gain control. Laza rested his hand on the open door, rocking it on its hinges.

We don't know what this is.

Yes, we do, and so do the Descendants.

Jocelyn stretched her muscles. They were tight from the constant fear haunting her. *Then what is it?*

It's a weapon.

Jocelyn shook her head. *I will not fight.*

You are young, and stupid, to believe you have a choice. The only option you have is which side you will choose.

The pain in her head pressed into her eyes and swollen nose.

Piean went to collect supplies and food. When she returns, I would like to discuss how I can help you.

The struggles of the day were taking their toll. Jocelyn's eyelids drooped, and she felt drowsy. She forced her eyes open. *And how are you going to do that?*

By bringing you to your grandfather.

The sleepiness was gone, replaced with an urge to know more. *You know where he is.*

Laza nodded.

Jocelyn's tail patted the water as she swam up from the mattress. *I would like to go now.*

Food first. Then we talk. Then we leave. It's a long journey, so rest.

Laza fluttered in the water, and Jocelyn sat back on the bed. She ran her hands over the sheet. It was tough and slick, nothing like the cotton on the ship, but it was still welcoming.

Laza began to swim through the door.

Wait! Jocelyn yelled.

Graying red hair fluttered in the water as the merman stopped in the doorway.

Do you think my grandmother is with him?

The smile slipped from Laza's mouth. *We don't know if she's still alive.*

The room spun. Jocelyn's stomach swelled with dread and nausea. *She was alive when she left me.*

Laza looked at the floor. *Then there's hope. Your grandmother is a smart merwoman.*

Jocelyn counted five chests among the clutter. *Am I your prisoner?*

Laza shook his head. *Oh no, child. You may leave if you wish, but I pray you don't.*

You chained me to a wall... She rubbed her sore wrist.

Imagine if I hadn't. You would've killed Piean and me. Then swam straight to Thessa and to the Descendants. You would have been lost before you could've been found.

Lifting off the bed, she kicked closer to him. The merman drifted aside, no longer blocking the doorway.

It is your choice.

Benlar shifted in the bed. The gunshot wound in his tail wouldn't allow him to sleep any longer. He sat up and grabbed a gray baleen shirt from the ground and pulled it over his head. The whale fabric was thick and heavy but strong.

He leaned over the bed and pulled out a large utility belt hidden beneath. Wrapping it around his waist, Benlar fastened the buckle. A second strap rested against his tail. With little thought, he quickly pulled the leather tight around his thigh and clicked the clasp together. A spasm tore through him. His wound throbbed under the pressure.

His fingers fumbled with the buckle. They weren't moving quickly enough. Benlar bit the side of his cheek to remind himself he was in charge of his body and not the pain. The release of the strap gave way to a long inhale of salt water.

This was going to be a nightmare.

Benlar loosened the belt. Cautious, he wrapped it once more around his thigh. The leather band hung too loose, but it would have to do.

He counted to ten, pushing the pain away, before lifting his crossbow from the table and pressing the pins holding it open. The weapon folded in on itself. He slipped it into one of the holsters attached to the belt. The short arrows went into a pouch on the belt that buttoned shut.

Lifting a flashlight, he flicked it on. The bright light shot to the ceiling. Turning it off, he untwisted the back. Two crystal tablets rested in the tubing. They would only last a few hours. He had to get more methane clathrate before the day's end.

He tucked the flashlight into his belt and picked up the knife.

Benlar pressed two levers on the handle with his thumb and index finger. The steel of the blade turned red from the internal electric burner. He moved his fingers from the triggers and waved the knife through the water, cooling it before sliding it into its scabbard.

Swimming for the door, he grabbed his money bag and tied it to a ring on his belt. The loose strap flapped against his thigh.

In the hallway, the open chatter of the crowd below echoed toward him. The open mind-talk gave him an instant headache. Concentrating, he blocked the voices and locked his door.

Mli was a smart girl, and she would stop here before moving on to Thessa. Or at least he hoped. He reached into a side pocket on his belt and pulled out a tintype picture of Mli. Her sweet eyes stared at him. Someone had to have seen her.

He swam down the hall to the lower floor. Merpeople crowded the small dining area, a few armed with crossbows over their shoulders. The once-dull wooden room had transformed into a colorful arrangement of clothing and fins. One mermaid swam from group to group, mingling above the seated guests. Her gold-speckled lace dress played with the light from the burning gas lamps. Hands waved around as some acted out what had happened to them during the freak storm. Except one.

A merman sat in the corner of the room, shifting his eye from one person to the next—searching. Benlar glanced at the guy for a brief moment before moving toward the bar, but that was all he needed to see the merman was trained in finding the hidden. Benlar counted two knives and a small crossbow on the guard's brown tail.

Benlar glanced at the floor and swam between the bodies and up to the bar. Every stool was occupied with confused merrows, searching each other for answers. The barkeep rested against the register. His eyes darted from guest to guest, eavesdropping.

Any idea what happened? Benlar asked.

The barkeep glanced at him and shook his head. *I figured you were a goner with the way the building shook on the third floor, but look at you. You even have a shirt on.*

Benlar couldn't stop a smile from escaping.

A merman with round spectacles pushed away from the bar to join a group of friends at a table. Benlar claimed the empty seat. The numbing pain stopped pulsating as his muscles relaxed under his silver scales. He flicked his tail to turn the chair toward the bar and brushed against a mermaid's red fin.

Sorry, Benlar said.

The young mermaid turned her head and glanced at him. Her black hair fell in ringlets around a tan face.

For a moment, Benlar was hypnotized by the young merwoman's beauty. But he shook it off.

The mermaid reached out her hand. *I'm Piean.*

Benlar shook her hand. Her palm was smooth. This girl didn't work in the mines.

Benlar.

So what brings you to Ommo? I doubt it's the fine cuisine.

The barkeep shifted. *We serve great food here.*

Piean's smile brightened her face. *Oh Led, you know I'm teasing you.*

A waiter rushed out from a swinging door beside the bar. A silver tray rested on his shoulder. The waiter carried the aroma of salted blue trevally around the room as he searched for the table to deliver the food to.

Benlar's stomach rumbled.

You might want to take this merman's order, Led. He looks famished to me. Piean leaned closer, directing her mind only to Benlar, and rested her hand on his thigh. Playing with the local boys was too easy. She wanted to see how this one would react to her. And the fact he was undeniably handsome was in her favor. *Are you hungry?*

Benlar was comfortable with ladies flirting with him, but the directness of this girl startled him. He searched to form a complete sentence but only managed to nod.

Good, she said.

Led leaned over the bar, resting his elbows between the two. He pulled out a white slate board from a shelf. A string tied a stick of graphite to the board.

Whatcha going to have?

Benlar focused on Led's hand, ready to write. *The trevally is fine.*

Yes, it is. Led scribbled on the board and pushed himself off the bar. *Do you want a drink?*

No, thank you. Benlar slipped Mli's picture onto the bar. He glanced back at the merman with the brown fin to make sure he wasn't looking his way before turning to Led and mind-talking only to him. *But I was curious if you might have helped this merwoman?*

Led glanced at the photo and shook his head. *Nope. And you're not the only one asking.*

What do you mean? Benlar asked.

A reward announced by Inam himself on that girl's safe return to Thessa has everyone searching for her. Even this morning I had a Thessian guard asking about her. She must be someone important.

How much is the reward? Benlar asked.

Four lives, the barkeep said before swimming through the swinging doors into the kitchen.

Shivers tickled Benlar's spine. A reward that high made no sense. Mli, the daughter of healers, no one important, sought after by the most powerful merperson in the sea. Nothing seemed right. His gut told him to keep his head low, find her, and hide her.

Piean walked her fingers over to the picture and took it from him. Her eyes locked on his. *Long-lost lover or just a sister?*

She winked at him as she lifted the picture to glance at the face. Her eyes narrowed as Mli's happy face stared at her. Her confident smile wavered, and heat rose to her cheeks. This boy was from Thessa.

Have you seen her? Benlar asked in a hushed voice.

A fake smile covered her uneasiness. *No.*

But the disguise was too late—Benlar knew she was lying. He grabbed her hand, pinning the photo between two fingers. *Where is she?*

Piean rolled her shoulders and lifted her chin. *I've never seen this girl before. Maybe you should ask someone else if they've seen your precious little girlfriend.* She slipped her small hands from his grasp. His touch was warm, and under other circumstances, she would've welcomed it.

Led swam out, carrying two burlap sacks from the kitchen.

Piean lifted from her chair and swung a tote over one shoulder. She swam to Led, kissed his cheek, and grabbed the bags of food.

From the corner of his eye, Benlar saw the merman in the corner glare at Piean.

Thank you. Tell Truo that I'll stop by next week, Piean said to Led.

Led grinned at the girl. *She would like that. And you tell Laza that his tab is waiting.*

Of course, she said.

Avoiding eye contact, Piean swam out of the building, leaving Benlar and the guard watching her.

Who is she? Benlar asked Led.

Led shook his head as Benlar turned toward him. *She's trouble. Always has been. The best advice is just to stay clear of her.*

Benlar sat up and kicked his tail, reactivating the aching pain. *Does she live nearby?*

Led's expression dropped into a frown. *Did you not hear me? Leave her be.*

I won't be needing the food, Benlar said, searching for his money bag, but all he found was an empty ring.

Like I said, she's trouble, Led said.

Camedia! Benlar glanced over at the merman, now playing with the handle of one of his knives. The merrow dropped a few coins on the table before drifting out the front door. Benlar turned to Led. *Do you have a back door?*

You know who he works for?

Benlar nodded.

Thessa's guards were the best trained in hunting of all the classes. If this merman was stalking Piean, then the girl had no fighting chance.

Led pointed to the kitchen door.

Benlar kicked to swim, but Led grabbed his arm before he could move.

The barkeep locked eyes with him. *He's looking for your girl too.* Led glanced at the photo of Mli in Benlar's hand. *You should hide that.*

Benlar did as told. *Thank you.* Benlar swam out of the room.

Aidan counted his leaden footsteps on the wooden deck. The air was thick and hot with little wind. He wiggled his nose at the smell of sweat from the thirty-two men staring up at him, waiting for him to open his mouth and speak. But Aidan's tongue was heavy, and his mind raced. How was he to explain a plan he didn't have? He couldn't expect this crew to give up their livelihood and morality to follow his selfish desire to stay on the ocean and find his love.

He twisted his fingers around the wooden pegs of the wheel and took in a deep breath. He stood tall, his eyes darting from one sailor to the next. Curiosity and sorrow from Jocelyn's departure into the sea weaved through the crowd. Aidan suspected they all had an inkling of what this meeting was about.

A young boy pushed his way through the stagnant crew. His oily auburn hair pressed flat to his head, and his eyes were wide but determined.

Aidan recognized the child and glanced at the lad's shoes. The oversized leather boots smacked as the lad took the first step to the poop deck and stopped. To see this child on deck was a rarity, for he seemed to live in the masts, soaring from one sail to the next as if he could fly.

The boy's hands twitched at his sides. Aidan glared at the frightened lad.

"Captain?"

The boy's name, George, rushed to Aidan's mind. The orphan who was abandoned in St. George Hanover Square with no name and no family.

"Yes, George?" Aidan asked.

The boy tightened his fists to stop them from twitching. "I be with you, sir."

A sad smile lifted Aidan's lips. This boy who had nothing but this ship would blindly give up his chance at a decent life.

"You haven't heard my proposal, young man." Aidan looked out at the rest of the crowd. Word spread fast on such a small ship, and Aidan could see the fear and respect on his crew's faces. "None of you have. Please, do not walk beside me until you know what is at stake."

Men shifted, allowing the breeze to flow between them. Thomas's steward, Mr. Marklee, stood in the mist of the crew with his arms crossed, listening.

"You be a man of justice!" A sailor yelled from the belly of the crowd.

"Hear, hear!" The crew cheered.

Aidan released the helm and marched to the stairs that descended to the mariners.

"Do not leap with such blind faith to a conclusion you assume is correct," Aidan shouted back at the men.

The happy spirit whisked away with the wind.

"I am not the captain you signed under anymore. I have no right to man this ship, for it has been revoked by Mr. Corwin and passed to my first mate, Mr. Gregory."

Aidan searched out Gregory at the back of the crowd. His first mate's face was ghost white as he listened.

"A fine man to take my place as your captain."

The roar of the men thundered as protests erupted. Sailors

glared at him, but Gregory stood his ground.

"You be our captain!" George screamed over the deafening voices.

"And that is why I stand here," Aidan said, walking into the crowd. The men parted, and their voices hushed to low whispers. "I am not a merchant captain anymore. I cannot and will not be returning to England as an honorable man, for if I do, I am to be accused, by your employer, of mutiny and murder."

A short man with balding hair inched his way to Aidan's right. "We could rid ourselves of Mr. Corwin before we reach London."

He faced the man. Breathing in the humidity, Aidan tried to cool his body. The heat from the men was suffocating.

"Then we would be murders, and have any of you heard of a decent outcome for a crew with a lost employer?"

A few men shook their heads.

Panic twitched in Aidan's gut. He needed fresh air. He made his way back. The breeze wrapped around him as he stepped on the stairs and stood next to George. Aidan looked at the child, around ten or so, with a button nose and large blue eyes. If this crew decided to follow him, what would happen to this child? Would he be stripped of his home on the ship, once again abandoned, or would he be forced to take to a life of uncertainty and danger? Would this be the start of a monster or a hero?

Aidan rested his hand on the boy's shoulder. The young lad's grin was contagious, and Aidan couldn't help but smile back. The wheel was spinning, and he couldn't stop it now.

Aidan addressed George and the rest of the men. "If you should remain under my leadership, you will be walking into the unknown. We will be deemed criminals and hunted. Many of you have families waiting for your return, and I do not expect you to join. I promise to return you safely to land with enough coin to see you home."

"To wot?" A deep voice echoed up to Aidan. "Wot I be understandin' is, we're out of employment if we leave this ship."

Aidan searched for the man but couldn't find him. "You will keep your good name, your work ethic, and will still be employable…"

"Wot do ye offer if we stay?" the same man asked over him.

The sweat on Aidan's palms cooled his skin. He wiped them on his breaches. "I can't offer you anything," he said.

The boom of voices shook against the calm surface of the ocean.

Aidan had lost his ship. His heart knocked against his ribs, trying to force its way out. If he wanted to stay on the ocean and out of jail, he had to do something.

"We have a ship, and we are damn good sailors. What I give you is an opportunity to break society's rules of class and order. A chance to prosper."

"With a stolen ship?" another crewmember asked.

"Yes!" Aidan left George and stepped up the stairs. He stared over his men. "Who better to pirate than a past merchant? Imagine what we could accomplish without the nagging of an employer. We have a ship with a burden already loaded. What I offer, sirs, is a chance to riches that you'll never acquire otherwise and the freedom of the ocean."

The crowd looked at each other, waiting to see who would act first.

Nicholas stepped from the group and stood beside George.

"As the boy said, I be with ye, Captain." Nicholas placed

his right fist over his heart.

One by one, twenty-six sailors did the same. Aidan nodded to each one, thanking them. His eyes stopped on Gregory who stood in the back. His first mate's sad eyes burned into his as he shook his head no.

The decision was done. Captain Aidan Boyd would be a pirate.

CHAPTER 10

The flames of the forever-burning streetlamps flickered within their glass domes. Benlar raced past them, searching for the mermaid with the red tail and the guard. His eyes darted from one side street to another. Each was empty. Everyone seemed to be indoors in case of another storm.

Dread filled Benlar's mind. She had taken everything *he* had saved for this journey. If he didn't retrieve his coins, he would be without a bargaining chip to find Mli. It would leave him no choice but to contact his family in Thessa. And at the moment, that would compromise his search.

He spun in the waters and glanced up at the defused sun in hopes of seeing the girl. The light beams played with the water, kissing it, leaving a golden hue on the moving ocean. Stone buildings towered over him, but no one was above him.

Turning over, Benlar swam higher to get a better view of Ommo. His tail kicked as adrenaline pumped through his veins. This mermaid knew this town and its hiding places, and he hoped that would keep the guard from finding her first.

Steam rose from copper pipes that lined the flat roof of the massive mine in the heart of the city. Millions of stacked stones formed the building. Hundreds of watermills encircled the large structure, each one turning full speed to keep the mine running.

Benlar surreptitiously studied the many faces coming and going from the colossal structure, but there was no dark-haired girl from the pub. Just merpeople wearing leather vests with tanks on their backs to protect them from the natural gases that leaked out.

Born into a landwalker bloodline, Benlar had been taught of the land above. He knew their languages, cultural differences, politics, and everything else he needed to know to blend in. He was great in his training and would have graduated top of his class if he hadn't set off to find Mli. To find his love, he had given up everything his family had worked for. He had broken every rule he had learned by walking out of the waters without orders.

A flash of a red fin beside a general store diverted Benlar's attention to an alley. The tail disappeared behind the rock building. No one else seemed to be following her.

His fingers curled into his palm as he kicked full speed toward his target. This Piean had no idea whom she was dealing with. He stayed high above the town, leaving a gap from his thief. She didn't seem the type to give up her secrets without a fight, and he had no desire to hurt a girl. Following her seemed the best solution. He glanced back to make sure he wasn't being followed. Only fish swam in the distance.

The mermaid darted from one alley to the next, glancing over her shoulder but never up. Benlar couldn't help but wonder how many times this mermaid had gotten away with stealing, and had she ever been caught, had her appearance allowed for gentle punishment, if any at all?

Her movements slowed as she approached an overgrown kelp forest on the outskirts of Ommo. Multicolored fish swayed in and out of the dark-green growth. Piean pulled the tote bag close to her and disappeared under the kelp fronds.

Benlar swooped down in the water. His eyes traced the ruffling seaweed. Keeping his distance, he swam low enough to take shelter if the girl should swim upward.

The tall stems of the kelp forest reached for the rays of sunlight filtering through the ocean in bright streaks. The warmth of the sun was diluted by the depth of the sea. Benlar's skin tingled at the memory of the hot sun beating down on him on land.

The heavy gravity had pinned him to the dirt as he'd crawled out of his home with just Mli's confused voice for comfort. He was jealous of the birds that soared above him. In the ocean he could fly, but on land he was stranded. The air burned his nostrils when he inhaled. The perfume of the honeysuckle and yellow roses had been the only tolerable thing from the world above.

The plants here smelled of salt.

The movement in the growth stopped. Benlar froze, searching for Piean. Minutes passed. He swallowed the ocean. She must know he was there.

Benlar kicked over to where Piean had disappeared. The leaves of the seaweed waved him toward their embrace.

An orange fish poked his head out of the greenery and stared up at him.

Piean? Benlar pushed his hands into the kelp and swam into the forest. The stringy leaves tickled his skin. *If that's even your real name.*

The orange fish trailed Benlar. It must've been someone's pet that swam off during the storm. Benlar reached out, and the fish darted into the gentle stroke. Definitely someone's pet.

Piean.

The fish took the lead, swimming to and fro in a giddy dance. Having company was agreeable, compared to the constant loneliness in Benlar's heart. Mli had been different when he'd found her. She was not the same girl he'd fallen in love with as a child. She had changed.

Camedia! Benlar circled in the water, looking for the mermaid. But he was alone, other than the fish swimming around his tail.

If he didn't find this girl, he would lose much more than his savings. He would lose his only lead to Mli.

He swam to the ground, pushing through the thick plants. She had to be close. His arms reached out. *Where are you?*

His new pet swam in front of him, darting around a protruding rock hidden in the seaweed.

Benlar stopped. There was something wrong with this rock. It was unnatural and bright in the low sunlight.

He pushed the kelp out of the way and grasped the silver handle. Hinges welded into the neighboring boulder held the door in place.

Lifting the heavy metal, he peered into the darkness that led deep underground.

This is where she went.

He pulled out his flashlight and turned it on. The remaining methane clathrate crystals would only last a few hours. Hopefully enough time to find this mermaid. Benlar turned his head to see if anyone was lurking in the forest, but the fish was his only companion.

He swam into the hole with the fish close behind and closed the door. With luck, the guard had lost interest in Piean and had turned his skills elsewhere.

Benlar's gut argued with this logic.

Thessa's guards were good at reading others, but

landwalkers were great at it. Benlar knew the merman had found his target and was waiting to strike when it best suited the mission.

Propelling himself through the dark water, Benlar swam fast. He had to get to Mli before anyone else did.

Piean rushed into the house with a pack pulled over her back.

The aroma of cooked seaweed and fish filled the home, drawing Jocelyn and Laza to the dining room. Piean dropped the tote onto the table and pulled out three nets filled with food. She passed one to Laza, then slid another to Jocelyn, avoiding any contact.

The smell was pleasing, but Jocelyn's stomach flipped at the thought of eating. She sat anyway and pulled open the dish. She needed energy, and food was one way to get it. The wilted boiled seaweed was pitiful compared to Piean and Laza's grilled fish. The sparkle in Piean's eyes made it clear she did it on purpose.

Jocelyn picked through the netting holding the cooked plant and examined the seaweed before taking a bite. The gritty flakes stuck to the top of her mouth.

Lad outdid himself, Laza declared as he feasted on his meal.

Shouldn't she be in the other room? Piean asked, her hand resting on the butt of her knife.

Don't be silly. She's our guest. Laza turned to Jocelyn and glanced at her net. *Eat, girl. You'll need your strength.*

She almost killed us, Piean piped up.

But she didn't.

Jocelyn smiled at Laza's remark. This crazy old merman was starting to grow on her.

Piean sat down and took a bite of her food. *How's your nose?*

The echo of delight in the mermaid's voice rang in Jocelyn's mind. She glared up at the young mermaid, grinding her teeth. *Fine. How's your head? It sounded like you hit it hard.*

Piean rolled her shoulders, lifting her chin. *Nothing I can't handle.*

Girls. Girls. Both of you are being ridiculous, worrying about the past. Don't you see you're on the same side?

Where is my grandfather? Jocelyn dropped her fist onto the table. The dull thud was nothing compared to the loud thud it would've made on land.

Eat.

I'm done eating. Where is he?

Laza wiped the corners of his mouth with a burgundy napkin. *He's a two-week journey from here with transportation. A month by tail.*

We're leaving? Piean's shock rang over the dinner table. *Are we going to Thessa?*

Laza grasped the flaky white meat in his net. *In good time.*

When?

Jocelyn sat back, allowing Piean to ask the questions.

Tomorrow. We have to make arrangements.

Jocelyn turned to face Laza. *What type of arrangements?*

We'll need transportation, supplies, and coin, and I need to retire my lab until I return. This all takes time, my dear. I also wouldn't mind standing on two legs for a bit before we leave.

The image of Laza with legs in the glass room popped into Jocelyn's mind. *How did you do that?*

Excitement widened Piean's eyes. *Laza was once a landwalker. I miss it.*

Being human? Jocelyn asked.

Don't you? Laza took a bite of his food.

Jocelyn's gaze darted between the two. *Does it matter?*

Laza squinted. *I would hope so.*

Why were you on land? Piean asked.

Picking her fingernails, Jocelyn peered down at her lap. *My grandmother thought it was the safest place.*

How? Nothing is safe on land, Piean said.

How else would she disappear from Fiar? If she were in the ocean, that merman would've found her, Laza piped up.

Jocelyn's heart dropped to her stomach as she remembered Fiar slicing her mother's neck, her dead eyes staring into nothingness. The last time Jocelyn had been near the merman, he'd injected her with a gas that had taken away her memories. The ocean's rage sent him catapulting through the sea— Jocelyn had prayed for his death.

Is he alive?

I assume so. He was reported at the last council meeting with the Descendants. On Inam's right-hand side, Laza said.

Jocelyn pushed her net away.

Eat! Laza ordered.

I'm not hungry.

You will die if you don't eat.

Piean took a bite. *You might as well do as he says. Otherwise, he'll nag you the rest of the day.*

I'm not hungry! Jocelyn shoved away from the table. *I want answers. I want to kill that merman! I want...* Her mind spun to Aidan's face.

You can't accomplish those things on an empty stomach. Eat. Laza pointed to her net.

Jocelyn did as she was told.

She wanted Aidan. She wanted to be out of this world and

by his side. Before, the medallion was her key to turning human, but now, she didn't know how to begin the transformation without the trinket. Laza and her grandfather were her only hope to ever see him again.

If they couldn't teach her how to be human, then all hope was lost.

Aidan rested his legs on an empty chair at the dining table. Memories of Jocelyn in the hideous purple dress with her hair pulled back too tight haunted him. He could picture her sitting in the chair where his feet rested.

Will it ever get easier?

He was pouring himself another glass of wine when the door cracked opened and Thomas walked into the room.

Thomas glided to a chair, the heels of his boots clicking on the wood floor. He flipped the tail of his coat before settling into his seat. His lips were pursed, eyes sharp.

The air thickened as the two men stared at each other.

"I heard you have control of the ship," Thomas said, pouring a glass of water into his crystal wine glass.

Aidan grinned at him. The power this man once welded had washed away with the rising tide. "I have," Aidan said.

Thomas's bloodshot eyes locked onto Aidan's. "And what is to be done with me?"

"I promise you, no harm will come to you or your man. We'll turn our course back toward India, where we will leave you."

Thomas ran his tongue over his teeth. "What about the burden?"

Aidan slid his feet off the chair and sat up straighter. "What about the cargo?"

"I would like a percentage." Thomas sipped his water.

Aidan smiled at his pompous company. This man with old money still clung to every half guinea his sweaty fingers could pinch. "Really? And what type of percentage are you speaking of?"

"Thirty percent," Thomas answered.

Aidan traced the top of his wine glass. "Thirty?"

"Yes. You need my name."

"But we don't need you for that, now do we?" Aidan leaned over the table, resting on his elbows. "You have no bartering chip here. You're lucky you're leaving with your life."

Thomas scratched his right eyelid, unaffected by Aidan's threat. "Yes, yes, you could kill me. We've all heard this before. But just listen."

Aidan sat back in his chair. Thomas was one to take control of any conversation, and he was curious what his ex-employer had to say. "I'm listening."

Someone knocked on the door. Aidan glanced over to the noise then back at Thomas.

"I would assume it's Mr. Marklee. I asked him to find me some wine. I seem to be out in my quarters," Thomas responded.

"Come in," Aidan said.

Mr. Marklee cracked open the door and walked in with his head low, holding a long-neck bottle.

"Leave it," Thomas ordered, pouring another glass of water. He inched closer to Aidan. "With you taking control of this ship, you have given me an idea. Leave me in India where I will report this ship stolen along with the cargo and supplies.

My insurance policy will cover my losses."

Mr. Marklee placed the wine bottle on the table and left, never making eye contact. Staying invisible.

"Of course," Aidan interrupted. "And where do I play in your scheme?"

"When you sell the cargo, I receive fifteen percent of the profit."

Laughter bellowed out of Aidan.

"You laugh because you don't see the bigger picture," Thomas said, standing. He paced the room, his eyes beaming with excitement. "When sale prices are low and there is no gain, you and your merry men will be pirates, and I..."

Aidan's smile faded. "And insurance will pay, and we'll pocket the entire profit."

Thomas was a brilliant businessman.

"I knew my father had taught you some business traits," Thomas said. "Thirty percent is mine, and you don't have to be a real pirate."

It was too simple. Thomas's plan would eliminate the law and provide a steady income to him and his crew, but at what cost?

"Twenty-five," Aidan said.

Thomas smiled as he poured his water onto the ground and filled the glass with wine.

"Done." Thomas sipped the alcohol. "Good thing, for Aidan Boyd is a horrible name for a pirate."

CHAPTER 11

The beam of Benlar's flashlight illuminated the small tunnel, disturbing sleeping shadows. Dark-green algae climbed up the smooth rocks surrounding him. He slowed his pace, swimming toward the core of the earth.

The pathway narrowed, and Benlar's shoulders scraped the cold walls. He focused on staying in a straight line. Whoever had created this tunnel was not claustrophobic.

His new pet swam in a playful mood ahead. Benlar ran his hand over the fish when he swam past it. The creature fluffed its bright-orange fins.

Benlar was never allowed to have pets in his home. With three sons and careers, his parents didn't have the time or the room in their hearts to take in any animals.

What are we to do with them? What is their purpose? Benlar's father had asked whenever the subject came up.

And Benlar had answered: *To be my friend.*

The way Benlar's father's upper lip curled with disgust still flipped Benlar's stomach.

Useless. You are strong because of you. Friends are a waste of time and potential risks. You know this, son. To rely on someone else is a deadly two-edge sword wielded by the blind. Someone will get cut.

Being born into a landwalker's family had certain privileges, but for Benlar, childhood was nothing more than slow torture. School and training took precedent. Love and comfort were viewed as unnecessary distractions. At seven, he was transported to a training camp for a year with no communication from home. There, he learned how to manipulate the weak with their own language, a silent glance, or if needed, his pheromones.

At first, the instructors had them use the chemical messengers with each other. Underwater, it was nothing more than a scent. Each one as unique as the individual. But on land, it was hypnotic.

The gray eyes of an old woman took away Benlar's youth. On his first trip to land, his assignment was to convince a human that he could walk on water and they could too. The old woman followed him into the rising tide, shivering. Her wrinkled hand reached for him, and he almost took it but stopped himself when he stared into her human eyes. Instead, he dove deep, leaving the woman. He was the first of his class to manipulate a human. The praises rang in his ears.

It got easier with each assignment. On land, Benlar played the humans' heartstrings with a beautiful melody. Each one followed without question, handing over everything they had. The training was about being superior.

When he had come home, he'd changed. No longer the child who needed a friend, but the boy who could conquer worlds. Head of his class, his parents paraded him around like a living trophy. *Our son, whose talents are better than yours.* Benlar's brothers hated him.

The only one who saw past the puppet show was Mli.

Why do you look sad? the young girl, still growing into her smile, had asked him the first time they met, her pet manta ray swimming around them.

I'm not, he answered.

She shook her head. *But you are. I can see it.*

Mli offered her hand, and he took it. From then on, his heart was hers.

Benlar ran his fingers over the semitransparent fin of his new companion. *Someone must be missing you.*

The dark eyes of the fish glanced at him.

His flashlight's beam reflected something at the end of the tunnel. Benlar kicked harder to get a clear view. A round, silver door blocked the end of the pathway, a leafless tree and star carved into the metal.

Benlar gripped the handle to the heavy entry and pulled, but it would not budge. It was locked from the inside. He had no choice. He raised his arm and banged on the door.

The color in Piean's face paled with each loud knock that pulsated through the water into the dining room.

Jocelyn watched the young mermaid's eyes dart from the money purse attached to her corset to the door.

Return it, Laza ordered in a shallow whisper.

I wasn't followed. Piean fidgeted with the purse.

Laza ate the last bite. *Obviously, my dear, you were. Just return whatever you stole. We don't have time for a quarrel with the locals.*

Jocelyn could taste Piean's anxiety dissolving into the ocean as she shifted in her chair. The girl was nervous, and Jocelyn loved it.

I don't think it's wise. They'll go away, Piean said.

I could answer it for you, since you've been such a delightful host.

Jocelyn pushed away from the table and dove toward the doorway.

Laza and Piean both shot up from the table, screaming, *No!*

You said I'm free, Jocelyn answered, swimming away from them. With food and sleep, her body sprinted through the water with ease. Piean and Laza were not as quick.

Jocelyn reached the banging door.

Piean! Open the door! A merman's voice boomed through the metal.

Jocelyn knew this voice. Her hand trembled as her fingers unlocked the door. She flung it open and threw herself into his arms.

Benlar's eyes opened wide in shock. His heart pounded in his chest. He didn't see her face when she'd embraced him, but he didn't have too. The way her body fit to his—it was his Mli.

He pulled away, looking her over. *Are you all right?* he asked, his voice laced with worry.

She nodded.

Benlar exhaled as he wrapped his arms around her, holding her. They sank to the floor. He kissed the top of her head. The orange fish swam in circles around them.

Jocelyn gave in to the solace he brought. This boy had been her bulwark through her childhood, protecting her from childish dangers. But this was different. This wasn't pretend, but she knew he could still keep her safe.

How did you find me? she asked.

Benlar stroked her spine through the seaweed shirt. *It was easy.*

The sarcasm made Jocelyn laugh. *Are you all right?* she asked, still not ready to let go of him.

Nothing I can't survive.

Jocelyn tilted her head toward Benlar's. He kissed her

forehead just as he had a thousand times before, but this kiss was different. Filled with sadness.

Let's go, Benlar pleaded. *You're not safe.*

Nowhere is safe. Laza's voice broke through their embrace, bringing their attention back to the strange home.

Benlar shoved Jocelyn behind him. The old merman was still in the hallway of the dwelling, too close. Benlar rolled his shoulders and swam tall, blocking Jocelyn from view. His new pet followed suit and darted behind Jocelyn.

Who are you? Benlar asked.

Laza reached out a hand, but Benlar kept his by his side. *I'm Doctor Laza, a friend of Mli's grandfather. In fact, we need to hurry so we can see him.*

Benlar moved his head to the side. *What?*

Laza dropped his hand. *Your arrival is going to delay us if we don't get moving, Mr. Benlar, son of Rockstin.*

Benlar released his knife from his belt and held it up, ready to fight. First rule of training: never trust someone who knows too much about you.

Jocelyn peeked over Benlar's shoulder at the weapon. The once-deadly blade seemed like a child's toy after the glimpse of her own ability. A power she didn't yet understand.

She touched Benlar's forearm. *He's right. We need to get moving.*

Benlar glanced at Jocelyn. His eyebrows pressed down.

They have answers I need. Jocelyn swam around Benlar and into the home. *Are you coming?*

Laza held open the door as Benlar entered the house, his blade ready to strike.

What do you mean, see him? Rumor is Helo died eight years ago, Benlar said, his fish staying close to him.

Laza closed the door and locked it. *Define dead.*

The figurehead of the ship peered up at the white clouds drifting in the blue sky. The warm ocean lapped against her tail.

Aidan's fingers tapped against the bow's rail. He studied the naked figure of human and fish, known as Neptune's wooden angel. Carved for the prow of his ship, she was a talisman for calm seas.

Lifeless eyes stared up at Aidan. Would she have to be returned to the sea? He reached down and traced the elmwood curves of her hair. If Jocelyn was a mermaid, did she look like this stiff creature? He lifted his eyes to the heaven.

"Please let her be a mermaid," he said to God above. If she wasn't, then he'd lost her forever. He pulled his hand away from the figurehead.

The reflection of the bright sun shimmered in the small ripples of the gentle sea. India's shore lined the horizon with a promise of a new beginning.

Aidan turned and faced *his* ship. His men skirted about, manning the boat. He would never have to return to land if he didn't desire. His home was the ocean, and from this moment, he would fight to stay with her.

He would be in India tomorrow and rid himself of Thomas. He walked toward the belly of the ship, his leather coat flapping in the wind. Before they reached land, Aidan needed to know everything about the mystical creatures he would be searching for, and he knew where to start. He climbed down the ladder to the pathway that led to the dining hall, where Nicholas would be eating.

CHAPTER 12

Burnt meat pies permeated the mess room. Aidan's hunger evaporated with the unpalatable aroma. The cook, Henry, mourned the loss of Jocelyn through raw or overcooked food, salted with his tears. Believing her dead, Henry had locked himself in the galley to peel potatoes, avoiding the crew for hours. Aidan's heart ached for the man, who acted as if he'd lost a daughter instead of an assistant.

The handful of sailors in the large room toyed with their food, pushing it around their plates. Green tinted most of their cheeks. But bad food was still food.

Nicholas sat in the corner of the large space. Without protest, he speared the over-salted beef with his fork and chewed the tough meat in loud, open-mouthed bites.

Hanging lanterns swayed with the rocking ship. The flame's warm glow blended with bright rays of sunlight, the smoke escaping through the grating of the upper deck.

The mess hall creaked with the ocean's pressure. Aidan walked the dull, long planks of flooring through the maze of wooden tables, hanging on thick ropes from the ceiling, and sat across from Nicholas.

The white-bearded man glanced up at his captain, then

back at his food. "This 'ere food tastes of piss. 'Ave ye eaten?" Nicholas took another bite.

"We need to talk," Aidan said, pushing Nicholas's plate away from the old man.

"I be figuring so. With ye being down 'ere and all."

"She said she was a mermaid." The word mermaid rolled off Aidan's tongue, leaving a foolish aftertaste.

Nicholas grabbed his dish and slid it back in front of him. He picked up the blackened biscuit and took a bite. The hard flour crunched under his teeth.

"Please, give me an answer."

Nicholas dropped the hard bread onto his square wooden plate. "Were ye asking me a question?"

Aidan ran his fingers through his dark hair, oil and sweat stuck to his skin. "Is she a mermaid?"

The old man's wild eyebrows scrunched inward. "'Ow can ye ask such a question? You of all men 'ave seen wot she be."

Resting his head on his hands, Aidan's upper body weighed down the hanging table. The heavy twine of the ropes pulled tight. "I don't know what I saw anymore."

Nicholas toyed with his fork, balancing it on his biscuit. "Do ye think she be alive, Captain?"

Aidan glanced up at his friend. "Yes."

"Do ye need more than that?"

"Yes. I need to know how to find her."

Nicholas laid down the fork. "Follow me," he said, standing. He walked out of the dining hall.

Aidan rushed after him.

The water mirrored the bright sun above. Aidan covered his eyes for a moment, adjusting to the light, as he stepped out of the belly of the ship.

Nicholas's short legs trudged across the deck to the bow.

The draft mark cut through the sea as a bell rang to call a shift change. Tired men sauntered past Nicholas and Aidan in search of a hammock.

"Look." Nicholas pointed to the land in front of them.

"What about it?" Aidan gripped the rail to steady himself.

"It be the wrong way." Nicholas pointed his finger toward the open sea. "If ye wish to find 'er, ye start there."

Aidan shook his head. His white shirt collected the humidity, trapping the heat against his skin. "We cannot sit idol, waiting."

Nicholas's dirty fingernails scratched at his beard. "She won't be on land, sir."

"She breathed air. She walked among us." Aidan shifted. "If she is a mermaid, then how could she do such things?"

"Do ye question the turtle who lives on land and water? We be nothing more than small rocks buried beneath the dirt, with very little knowledge of above."

Aidan slammed the palms of his hands on the rail. "Why must you talk in riddles? Speak clear, man, for I don't have time for this. For her sake and mine, tell me what you know."

"Do ye believe in mermaids, Captain?"

"I don't know," Aidan said, frustration tinging his voice.

"Yes, ye do." Nicholas grabbed his knife from his belt and pierced the wood railing.

"What are you doing?" Aidan yelled, reaching for the blade.

The old man was finished before Aidan could take it from him. A circle, three waves connected together, a small triangle in the center, was carved into the dark wood.

"Ye know wot ye saw." Nicholas shielded his blade in its leather cover.

Aidan had witnessed the gears of the burning medallion,

with the same symbol Nicholas had carved into his ship, spin as the copper metal fused into Jocelyn's chest. Her yellow-tinted eyes had turned black before she hit the water. It had changed her.

"Could it change me?" he asked Nicholas.

The old man's downcast smile gave Aidan his answer. "Ye can never be from the sea."

"Can I ever be with her?"

Nicholas patted his captain's shoulder. "That would depend on her and wot she chooses. But I would prepare yerself to protect yer heart, sir. Mermaids are known to break 'em."

Sit. Laza pointed at the table with the scattered nets.

Benlar complied, taking the chair next to Jocelyn. His hand never left the handle of his blade.

The pet fish didn't take long to trust Laza. It swam around the old merman's head then around the space, exploring.

It was a large, windowless room. Floral designs adorned the walls in a golden foil that caught the light. Without the gas-lit chandelier and hanging lanterns, it would've been pitch dark. Benlar swallowed back the urge to swim away. This place reminded him of an eternity box the humans used to bury their dead deep in the ground.

When was the last time you ate, Mr. Benlar? Laza asked, clearing the nets.

I'm fine, Benlar said.

The old merman set down a net-covered bowl in front of his guest.

You look horrible. We must keep up your strength. Laza glanced around the room. *Where did that girl go?*

Jocelyn weaved her hand through Benlar's. His warmth heated the water near her. *What happened?* she asked.

Above?

Jocelyn nodded, turning her tail to face him.

Nothing eventful, really. Just a lot of talking.

Jocelyn leaned closer. He was a good liar, but not great. *How did you get off the ship?*

Benlar squeezed her hand tighter, not willing to let it go again. *Your Mr. Boyd threw me overboard.*

She bit her lip at Aidan's name.

She couldn't love him. He wasn't from the ocean. Benlar tried to convince himself.

Were you hurt? she asked.

There she was. His sweet Mli, taking care of him. He smiled and kissed the top of her hand. His black eyes traced her face, stopping on her nose. *Camedia! What happened to your face?*

Jocelyn touched her nose, confused for a second. The adrenaline of seeing Benlar had masked the pain from the fractured bone and bruising for a moment.

I broke it, Piean said, swimming under the doorframe.

Laza glared at her. *Where have you been hiding?*

I haven't been hiding.

Benlar tilted his head at the old merman. *You might want to hide your coin flap before she disappears again.*

Laza beamed at Piean. *She is truly talented. When I found her, she was nothing more than a thrown-out doll. Now she is something fierce.*

Jocelyn mocked Laza's expression. *A true lady.*

I believe I am, Piean said as she swam into the room. She moved with grace through the water, shakiness substituted with confidence. Dropping a coin purse on the table, she slid it to Benlar with a painted fingernail. *You might want this back.*

Benlar squinted. *Do I need to count it?*

Piean smirked. *I would.*

Jocelyn studied the mermaid's face. The candlelight rolled off Piean's tan skin in a warm glow, brushing her full lips. Jocelyn may have hated the girl, but she couldn't deny her beauty. It made her uncomfortable.

A guard from Thessa followed you, Benlar said.

Laza sharp stare landed on Piean. *Excuse me?*

Piean rolled a strand of hair in her fingers. *He wasn't hard to lose.*

You don't just lose a guard, Benlar said.

You two have met, then? Jocelyn asked, slipping her hand out of Benlar's.

For a moment, Piean said. Her eyes stayed focused on Benlar's. *I'm glad you found your girlfriend.*

Benlar sat back in the chair. His cheek flinched with amusement. *Me too.*

Clenching his hands, Laza breathed in and out. *Where?*

The mine. Just as you showed me. He has no idea what happened to me, Piean said.

Laza's face lit up. *Then we are fine.*

I found you, Benlar said, fastening the coin purse to a ring on his belt.

Piean sat down and nodded. *I guess I wanted you to. You really should eat. You look appalling.* She reached for the net of meat.

Benlar shot forward, pinning Piean's wrist to the table. The mermaid gasped.

Laza studied from a safe distance.

Jocelyn sat still, unstartled by Benlar's rash movement. She knew him better than he knew himself, and his temper continued to be his downfall. She sat back, watching.

No one steals from me. Benlar's deep tone echoed through everyone's mind.

Digging her fingertips into the wood, Piean lifted her hand, but Benlar pinned it back down. Her upper lip twitched.

Trained to be fast, Benlar retrieved the knife from his belt in a mere second and pointed the burning tip in Piean's direction. *And no one touches Mli!*

The fish darted around Benlar in a frantic swim.

I like it rough. Piean mustered a smile.

Laza rolled his eyes as he swam over to the table. *Now what are you going to do? Kill us all?* He sat and stared at Jocelyn. *Is that what you wish him to do?*

I don't need him to kill you. I'm quite capable, Jocelyn said, digging her fingers into the netting on the bowl. Gray pieces of fish meat floated in the glass container. She snagged one and rolled it between her fingers before eating it.

Partially, dear. Laza covered the dish. *Put the knife away.*

No, Benlar said, holding tight to the blade and Piean.

Laza made eye contact with Jocelyn. *We really don't have time for these games.*

Benlar, please put the knife down, Jocelyn said.

Benlar did as she asked.

Jocelyn pushed away from the table and punched Piean. Benlar jumped, letting go of Piean's hand.

Both girls screamed. Jocelyn held tight to her throbbing fist, while Piean held her cheek.

Camedia! Piean yelled at Jocelyn.

Jocelyn's eyes glimmered through the pain. *We're even. Next time you cross me, I won't just hurt you. I'll kill you.*

Benlar flinched at the darkness in Jocelyn's voice.

Well, that was fun. Laza lifted himself from the table. *We should pack if we want to leave by tomorrow. Mr. Benlar, you might wish to retrieve your possessions.*

Benlar shook his head. *Not unless she's going with me.*

Then you'll have to live with what you have on, Laza said.

Don't worry about me, Benlar stated.

The old merman smiled. *I don't have time for that.*

Piean sat, covering her face with her hand, avoiding conversation.

Jocelyn hoped her lack of interest was from fear.

Laza pushed the food toward Benlar. *Eat, boy. Tomorrow will come quick.*

CHAPTER 13

The afternoon dwindled to evening as the setting sun faded over the ocean. Vibrant purple, pink, and orange clouds held tight to the dimming light. One by one, thousands of stars gave life to the sailor's way home. Aidan counted ten of the tiny suns before losing himself to the emptiness of space, alone in his world.

The rhythm of holystone scraping against the floorboards, accompanied by the low-pitched creaks of the moving ship, brought a tranquil slumber over the boat and her crew. Even the rambunctious boy, George, moved in a slow dance with his mop—his eyes half closed in a daze. Aidan could compose a symphony with the recurring noises of a working ship.

He brushed loose strands of hair from his face. The small night crew of sailors manned their stations on the upper deck. Aidan could feel their eyes glancing at his back, but each one kept his distance. Tomorrow was coming quick. Bored English gentlemen thrived on gossip, and with the *Clíodhna* redocking in Calcutta, rumors would spread until they reached the homeland.

Christened *Clíodhna* by Baron Christopher Corwin himself, after the Irish goddess of love and beauty and for the ship's unique elegance, she was destined for a long, prosperous life of law-abiding work. Sadness inched its way into Aidan's heart. His mentor believed he would do great things, but with the turn of the moon, Aidan's bright future had darkened with the night.

Aidan ran his finger over the carved indent of Jocelyn's medallion Nicholas had created. Something so small separated their worlds. He'd hidden the trinket from Jocelyn, hoping to give it to her as a token of his love. Unwittingly, he'd given her extra time as a human.

The bearish clearing of a throat interrupted the soothing lull of the sea. Aidan peered over his shoulder, his hand covering the symbol.

His business partner clenched his teeth on a clay pipe. The embers of the burning tobacco glowed red as Thomas inhaled. He exhaled—smoke clouding his face for a moment before whisking away into the ocean breeze.

"When we set foot on soil, we need to have a solid story. No missing girl…"

"Jocelyn," Aidan interrupted Thomas.

The pipe titled down with the pressure of Thomas's jaw tightening. "Of course. Miss Jocelyn is resting in her chambers, and we are here due to spoiled goods."

"Will that not cause a dispute with our traders? They will want to keep their good reputation."

Thomas removed the pipe from his mouth. "Would you rather tell the truth?"

"Of course not. It's just…won't it bring unwanted attention?"

Tapping his pipe on the rail, Thomas sent the burning remains of the flaked tobacco into the black waters. The last of the rum-flavored smoke swirled in Aidan's nose.

"No matter how we spin this, everyone's eye will be on us. We did not leave on the simplest of terms."

"No we did not," Aidan responded.

"At least I had the good sense to pay our remaining tabs before your rushed departure."

The bitterness in Thomas's tone flicked at Aidan's eardrums. He took a step forward, invading the man's personal space. He still had time to throw him overboard.

"She was dying."

"So you swept her to the ship to sail where? Who was going to save her out there?" Thomas tilted his chin toward the sea.

"You don't understand," Aidan said, frustration boiling under his skin.

Thomas toyed with his pipe. "Do I not? Jealousy is a strange beast. She was never going to choose you."

Aidan's hand dropped from the rail. His eyes widened.

"Don't puff your chest out just yet. I don't believe she would have chosen me either. With Mr. Benlar present, neither of us would've taken her home."

Aidan's shoulders slumped. There was truth to what Thomas said. Would she have chosen him with Benlar near her?

"Quite a pity she's dead. She was a beautiful thing. Especially her eyes."

Aidan peered at Thomas's dark eyes. Heat rushed down his neck, to his back. "She's not dead," he whispered.

Thomas shook his head. "Don't be delusional."

"She's not dead!" Aidan shoved Thomas. The clay pipe dropped to the ground, and the stem broke.

"Damn it, man!" Thomas yelled, pushing back.

Aidan couldn't control his temper, and he swung, but

Thomas was quick. He ducked and socked Aidan in the gut. The breath rushed out of Aidan. Panic settled in as he gulped for the air he'd lost.

Thomas rose, whipping his sandy blond hair from his face. "If you are going to swing first, make sure you know how to win."

The sailors' movements stopped as they all focused on Aidan and Thomas. Their judging stares pierced Aidan's skin. If he was to keep these men's respect and fellowship, he had to do something. Grounding his foot, he shoved off and into Thomas, bringing them both to the ground.

Thomas's bony elbow pounded into Aidan's shoulder blade. Aidan grunted with the sharp pain. He pulled back his arm and punched Thomas in the chest.

The crash of Thomas's fist crunched across Aidan's face. Adrenaline invaded his blood, dulling the pain. Relief washed over Aidan as he swung again. He pictured Jocelyn holding tight to Benlar—he swung. Her eyes turning black—he swung. Her sinking into the ocean—he swung. And with every punch he received, Aidan welcomed the pain.

The two of them continued to throw punches, rolling around the wet deck. Sailors circled them, cheering.

Small hands reached between the two and pushed. George's short body soon wedged between Thomas and Aidan. "Someone grab 'em!" the boy screamed above the cheers.

A few men did as told and separated their captain from his enemy.

Aidan panted. He couldn't help but smile at Thomas's disarray. His perfect clothes were torn and wrinkled. His lip bled profusely.

"Do you feel better now?" Thomas asked through grinding teeth.

Aidan blinked. He was lighter. Refreshed. The anger eating him from the inside was gone. He wiggled out of his men's grip. "Let him go," he ordered.

The sailors did what they were told.

Thomas lifted his chin, authority radiating from him. But the effect was lost on Aidan.

"Should we talk business?" Aidan asked, fixing his tousled clothing.

Thomas's eyebrows drew together. "You should be arrested!"

Laughter bellowed from Aidan. "We both needed the exercise. Come on, let's discuss India." He reached out and patted Thomas's shoulder. The man flinched.

"India?" Thomas wiped his lip, smearing blood.

"India," Aidan answered.

The house was packed. Every room was stripped of valuables, hidden from anyone who might find their way down here. Bags and chests lined the hallway. Laza and Piean heaved another large chest from Jocelyn's room.

Why do you need this? Piean asked, her breathing labored.

Benlar and Jocelyn sat on the bed, watching the two work. Benlar's pet slept next to his hip.

I already told you. They might be needed, Laza answered.

They're dead weight. Things already in your head, old man, Piean said.

My dear, my memory can't retain all of this information. We will need them. Laza dropped his side of the chest, the weight pulling Piean down with it.

Hey! she yelled.

Benlar, you should offer to help your elder. Laza's gaze rested on the two.

I don't work for you, Benlar answered, holding tight to Jocelyn's hand.

How do you know? Laza rebutted. Rubbing his hands, the old merman sat on the chest. *We leave at first light. There is no time to waste on a power struggle. You are a very capable young merman, and we need your help.*

Jocelyn turned and looked at Benlar's glowering face. *We should help.* She focused on him only and whispered to his mind.

Benlar peeled his scowl away from Laza and peered at her, his green eyes gone. Jocelyn stared at her reflection in his black eyes. He was handsome.

Fine, he said, letting go of her.

Benlar pushed off the bed, swam over to the chest, and lifted it. The fish sprang awake, following him. Jocelyn watched Piean lift an eyebrow at Benlar's display of strength.

Piean ran her hand over the orange fish. *You have a pet fish? Sexy.*

He found me. Where do you want this? Benlar asked.

By the front door with the other luggage, Laza said.

Benlar swam out of the room with the fish in tow.

Good boy, Laza muttered, swimming over to Jocelyn.

What else do you need packed? Jocelyn asked. She picked at her golden tail, pulling up scales until they hurt. Then she released them, moving to the next row.

You, child, need to rest. The old merman sat next to her. *You should sleep.*

Piean fluttered in the water, reminding Jocelyn of the captured fish pulled from the ocean and slammed on the deck of Aidan's ship—not sure what to do or where to go.

Jocelyn straightened her back. *You said I'm wanted in Thessa. Why?*

Because of who you are, Laza answered.

Jocelyn's eyes found his. *And who am I?*

Piean's fidgeting stopped, and she too waited for the answer. Jocelyn could feel the girl's quickened heartbeat through the ocean water. *Thump. Thump. Thump.* Her own mimicked the rhythm.

Helo should explain, Laza answered, patting her tail.

Jocelyn shook her head. *You will answer.*

Benlar swam back into the room, his silver tail catching the light of the flickering, enclosed flame of the gas lanterns. *What's next?*

Everyone ignored his presence, focusing on Laza.

Answer me! Jocelyn yelled, the water thickening around her.

Laza's deadpan expression gave nothing away. *I can't.*

Why not? Jocelyn asked.

Because I don't fully understand what you are. But I know you are not one of us.

Benlar inched forward, but Piean reached out to stop him. She shook her head before staring at the two on the bed.

A mermaid? Jocelyn inhaled deep, the warm water rushing through the thin skin covering her gills.

No, he answered. He fished out her medallion from his vest and handed it to her.

Benlar's eyes widened. He hadn't noticed Mli's chest was missing the medallion. His tail gave way under him. *How is that possible?*

Jocelyn ran her fingers over the copper wiring of her medallion.

She's the only true mermaid, Laza responded.

Jocelyn glanced up from the trinket resting in her palm. *If that's true, then what are you?*

Laza tilted his head to the side and looked at her. *Human.*

CHAPTER 14

Jocelyn stared at the rock ceiling most of the night. She could sense Benlar doing the same. His measured breaths were a reminder she wasn't alone.

He'd insisted on sleeping near her. Piean brought heavy blankets and watched as he made a bed on the hard floor next to Jocelyn's mattress. His pet fish rushed to cuddle under them.

In the past, they'd shared private moments holding hands, kissing, and embracing. Passion had almost pushed them to the point of no return, but something had always stopped her. What if her heart knew more than her mind? Giving herself to Benlar would only cause unbearable heartbreak. He deserved more.

She loved him when she was a child and still loved him today. But she also loved Aidan with a different part of her heart. A human who'd fought for her. Who showed her she could belong above water. Jocelyn rolled over to face the wall. Would she ever see him again? And if she did, what would happen? With no memory of what she was, she had no control over her abilities. Did she trick him into falling in love with her? Was it ever real?

Jocelyn bit her bottom lip as she played back in her head Aidan's body pushing against hers in the pathways of the ship. Their lips touching. Hearts racing. The kisses were never long enough, only lasting for brief moments of privacy, which were few on a crowded ship. But were those moments nothing more than a lie she'd tricked herself into believing?

Benlar rustled under his blanket. He was here, and there was no question of manipulation. He had loved her before he'd disappeared from her mind.

Her brain ached, her mind spinning. Could he love her for who she was now? Did she want him too?

Weighing her down from floating up, the heavy blanket felt like a thousand hands pinning her down. Jocelyn couldn't kick it off quick enough.

Are you all right? Benlar asked, his voice warm and calm.

There was no use in lying; he would know. *No. I'm no different here than on land. I still don't know who I am.*

You're Mli. You'll always be Mli.

Jocelyn peered over the edge of the bed. Sewn-in rocks kept the seaweed-filled mattress from rising to the surface.

But I'm not. I was Jocelyn for so long, I lost the part of me who was Mli. I'm different. Dangerous.

Benlar shoved off the blanket and swam to her side. He gathered her into his arms. The small fish didn't stir from its hidden place under the blankets.

Those are just names. Bad things happened, and you have grown from them, but who you are now is who you have always been. Mli or Jocelyn, you are still the same unique girl.

But I'm not, Jocelyn thought to herself.

He needed her to be both. She breathed deep. Being in his arms, she remembered the naive Mli who still had parents waiting for her at home.

Nothing terrible could or would happen in his arms.

She stretched up and kissed his cheek. *Thank you.*

Benlar glanced down at her. *Of course,* he said, kissing her forehead.

With little thought, Jocelyn reached up and kissed his lips, just as she'd done a thousand time before. Benlar kissed her back, hunger behind his touch.

She pulled back. The room spun. *Will you lie with me until morning?*

Benlar nodded.

They lay back on the bed. Jocelyn rested her head on his chest, listening to his beating heart.

He'd lied to her, even if he didn't know it. She was dangerous, but for now, she was tired. Sleep pulled her eyelids down as Benlar brushed her hair with his fingers.

The feather mattress smelled of honeysuckle and broom petals. It smelled of her. Aidan tried to ignore the reminder that Jocelyn had once slept where he now lay, but it was useless. When he closed his eyes, he saw hers. Aidan kicked the blanket to the floor and sat up.

Arching his back, he stood, his white linen shirt hanging around his thighs. Aidan grabbed his folded buckskin breeches from the chair and slipped into them, tucked in his shirt, and buttoned up. His bare feet paced the room. The wear of the past few days weighed down his shoulders, and his body ached from lack of rest.

He rolled his neck. His tender joints popped with each rotation. With India soon upon them, he needed a clear head.

Aidan pulled his pillow and bedclothes from the bed and threw them on the ground, then raised the flat mattress to its side. The bed's rope platform crisscrossed the length of the frame. Aidan flipped the mattress over. The frame creaked from the burden.

Lying on the bed, he inhaled. Hints of her intoxicating scent bled through the layer of cotton and feathers, and Aidan curled into a ball. The cold, silver moonlight blanketed him. He shivered even though the room was warm.

Reaching his hand to the ground, he pulled the blanket up and over him. His warm breath thickened the small space. Lavender soap aroma filled his senses. Thankfully, all the linens and clothes had been washed and loaded on the ship before they'd departed India the first time. Otherwise he and his crew would've had only the clothes on their backs.

Tomorrow, they would anchor the ship and row to shore. A handful of crewmembers would secure more livestock and water for the journey with as little questioning as possible.

Aidan slipped his foot out of the hot blanket. The warm air brought relief, but he wasn't ready to emerge completely. He closed his eyes, and his muscles relaxed as his dream took form. Jocelyn's blue eyes turned black, and she kissed him to sleep.

CHAPTER 15

A gentle knock on the door woke Jocelyn from her slumber. Her head rested on Benlar's chest, his arms wrapped around her. Her body pleaded for more sleep as another knock invaded the room.

There's no time to dawdle. Laza's voice echoed in her mind.

Jocelyn gazed up at Benlar. His dark eyes stared at the ceiling.

I hear him, Benlar said.

She lifted her head and peered at him. *Did you get any sleep?*

A faint smile lifted Benlar's cheeks. *A little, but you slept well. I did.*

Do you trust them? Benlar asked, running his fingers through the tips of her hair.

Jocelyn shook her head. *No, but that merman knows things about me. And if he knows where my grandfather is…*

You don't really believe that, do you?

Jocelyn watched as the fish swam around the books on the shelf, rubbing its side on the rough binding. *That he's alive?*

The mattress shook with Benlar's nod.

I hope so, she said.

Do you think he can help you?

I don't know of anyone else who can, Jocelyn said. *I just need someone to explain to me why I can do what I do.*

Like what? Benlar asked, wiggling to sit up.

Jocelyn did the same, but before she could recline against the cold wall, Benlar pulled her close to him. *I feel the ocean. Hear it. Sometimes, control it.*

Can you now? Benlar's voice was lined with disbelief.

I can.

Show me.

Jocelyn picked at the blanket. *I can't. When it happens, I don't know who is stronger, the ocean or me.* She pulled away to study his face. *I know I sound crazy.*

Benlar ran the back of his hand down her face, then found her hand and took it. *I believe you.*

I need to go with them.

I will follow you.

Jocelyn leaned back against Benlar. *Thank you.*

You know I love you.

Jocelyn's heart froze. *I know.*

An awkward silence settled over the room. Benlar's body tightened as he waited, but she couldn't give him what he wanted.

He exhaled. *Can you believe the bit about us being humans? The old merman's insane. Every history book proves we descended from them, but we are not human anymore. We have evolved. Look at the Descendants...*

I've never seen them, Jocelyn interrupted.

Never?

No. There was no point. My parents worked all the time, and my grandparents — Jocelyn paused. *They never liked them. I've never been to Thessa.*

Remember your grandfather's lectures?

He was a good teacher.

Yes, he was. Do you think Laza knows where he is?

Jocelyn nodded. *He knows the story of the mage and fish.*

So? Every child does.

Jocelyn glanced around the room. *But Laza knows my grandfather's version. The one with a child from the sea.*

A loud knock erupted from the door.

The transportation is here. Piean's irritated voice fluttered in. *Do you think you two could help?*

Benlar kissed the top of Jocelyn's head. *Sure,* he answered, openminded. *I also need to make sure a boy gets his fish back.*

Benlar slipped away from Jocelyn and out of the blankets. The playful fish darted from his hands.

Did you name him? Jocelyn asked.

You know me and pets. I don't get attached, he said.

Jocelyn ran her hand through her hair. It was a tangled mess. *Yes, you do.*

Benlar smiled at her. *Are you ready?*

Jocelyn shook her head. *But there's no other choice.*

Of course there is. We can leave, hide.

Jocelyn tilted her head. He knew more than he'd told her. *When did Thessa start looking for me?*

He licked his lips. *The first notice for your return was three days after you said goodbye.*

Jocelyn pulled her tail from under the blanket. The ocean lifted her from the mattress in a gentle embrace. *Who made the request?*

Benlar's eyebrows turned inward. *Inam.*

Jocelyn's heart leaped in her chest. If he was after her, then there was nowhere to hide.

Inam? she repeated.

Benlar nodded. *There is a reward for your safe return.*

I don't understand, she said.

The door pushed opened. Laza and Piean drifted on the other side of the threshold. Piean looked ready to kill, and she had easy access to the many weapons strapped to her belt. Her hair was pulled back in a tight bun. Laza wore the same vest with a blue seaweed shirt under it.

We need to go, Laza said.

How much is the reward on my head? Jocelyn asked the group.

Piean swam in front of the men. *Four lifetimes.* She dropped a brush and scissors into Jocelyn's hands. *That's why we need to change what you look like.*

The anchor hit sand, the jolt reverberating through the thick chains to the wheel turned by six sailors. The calm, light-blue waters lapped around three lowered rowboats. Two were filled with crates of livestock. Each container held one dead animal, giving the illusion of sickness. Aidan hoped this was enough for a quick and silent trade. No livestock merchant wanted rumors of sickly animals. In the last ship, Aidan sat next to Gregory and the other men who'd chosen to stay in India with Thomas. Each one held a coin purse filled for their silence, paid by Thomas.

Aidan couldn't stop the unnerving tingling in his chest as he looked at each man. If any of them spoke, a British army would come for him and his crew.

His first mate tapped his foot. "You don't have to do this," Gregory said, the coins clinking together from his shaky hands.

Aidan smiled at him. Gregory had always been a little nervous. "I'm afraid I do," Aidan answered.

"There is no happy ending in what you're choosing."

"I know." Aidan lifted his hand to Gregory. "Thank you for being a friend."

Gregory took his hand and shook. "And you, mine."

Glancing around the boat, then at the two other watercraft, Aidan's eyes fell on Thomas, who sat in the front of one of the boats carrying livestock. His servant, Mr. Marklee, sat next to him. Thomas's overly large navy-blue hat deemed him more pompous than without it. A purple and blue bruise contoured the swelling under his left eye. His split bottom lip puffed out. Even though he looked beaten up, no one would question if he was the winner of the fight. He sat straight with his chin slightly turned toward the sky. Proud. He gave Aidan a quick nod.

Aidan complied. "Row, men. India waits."

Sailors took oars and drove them into the sea, pushing toward the shore of Calcutta, India.

CHAPTER 16

The chest Benlar carried scraped against the sides of the tunnel, chipping away settled dirt. Jocelyn swam close to the ground. Heavy bags filled with unknown supplies hung from her shoulders. Short strands of black hair tickled her cheek. She whipped them away with her shoulder. The ends of her once-long hair barely touched the base of her neck.

Only an hour ago, Piean had tied Jocelyn's long auburn hair into a ponytail and cut. The long silver scissors struggled to hack through the thick locks, leaving a jagged mess. Piean's eyes gleamed as she lathered Jocelyn's head with black octopus ink.

There, no one will notice you now, Piean had said, rubbing the ink from her hands with a handful of sand.

Jocelyn knew it was bad. She'd avoided any reflective surfaces as they packed, afraid of what she would see. Before she closed the door to her borrowed room, she stuffed her loose ponytail beneath the mattress. She didn't want anyone to find it floating around the chamber.

Laza led the way down the tunnel. His white tail flicked the water at a slow pace. His body was old and weak. This merman needed to go into hibernation.

The process of de-aging was simple but long. Rejuvenation took months in an induced coma, locked away in a pod. Large amounts of genetically altered cells, originating from a *Turritopsis dohrnii*, the immortal jellyfish, pumped through IVs into the sleeping body. Transdifferentiation occurred, and cells reversed their development. The longer a merperson remained in the pod, the younger they became. It also helped with healing wounds and sicknesses.

When Jocelyn turned eight, she'd learned of the hibernation procedure. Her grandmother left for a month, and when she returned, her hair was still gray, but the wrinkles were gone and her eyes were clear. She looked thirty years younger, even though she'd just celebrated her three hundred and thirty-second birthday.

Studying Laza, Jocelyn estimated six months would bring him back to his twenties. She couldn't help but wonder how many times he'd hibernated, or if he was even allowed. Jocelyn glanced at her own young hands, encircled by bracelets of blue and purple bruises. Still new, she had never been in hibernation. She was eighteen, but she felt older and tired. How long until age took over?

Pay attention! Piean's voice yelled at her.

One of the bags she carried dragged on the ground, lifting sand into the water. Jocelyn looked over her shoulder. Piean brushed sand grains out of her face.

Sorry, she said, lifting the bag.

Swimming behind Benlar, Jocelyn watched the pet fish dance around him. No way was this fish going to swim home voluntarily. It had fallen in love with him.

A door swung open, and the dark water lightened to a clear blue. Benlar held the chest close to him and squeezed through the round doorway. Jocelyn followed, clinging tight to the bags, and swam through the opening.

Inhaling, Jocelyn could breathe again. Freedom tasted sweet.

Defused sunlight from the surface one hundred and fifty feet above twinkled beside her. She turned to face a large water vessel. A round glass dome covered the front of the fish-shaped vehicle, held together by rusting copper plating and protruding bolts. Jocelyn had never seen such old machinery.

Will it run? Jocelyn asked.

Of course, Laza answered. *This beauty was made to last forever. Unlike the new vessels you need to replace every twenty years. Money scam.*

Money drives people, Benlar said.

No, son. Life does. Laza unlocked the door of their transportation. Flakes of rust dropped from the groaning hinges.

Jocelyn looked around her. With Ommo half a mile away, they were alone but exposed.

Benlar's fish raced around him, glad to be in the open. Benlar dropped the trunk to the ground and grabbed the dancing fish. He ran his fingers over the thin skin of its upper back fin.

You need to go home, Benlar said to the fish.

The creature buried itself in his hands. Benlar glanced at Jocelyn. His boyish eyes pleaded to keep his new pet, but his shoulders rolled back and he stood tall, every bit a merman.

Go! he screamed at the fish, who shrank in fear.

Its orange fins fanned the water, kicking away from Benlar and turning toward Ommo. It swam away.

I'm sorry, Jocelyn said.

He's safer here, Benlar said, lifting the chest. *Get in. We don't need anyone noticing you.*

She did as told and entered the vessel.

Most of the luggage and chests, brought to the ship earlier, were piled in two neat rows in the back belly of the submarine, leaving space for a door that led deeper into the vessel. The large, round room held everything a reading room would hold. Six red coral chairs encompassed a square table in the center of the space. An octopus sculpture dangled from the ceiling. Its tentacles stretched out, holding eight unlit lanterns. Gold and burgundy tiles covered the cold metal of the machine's floor. Three portholes lined each wall, allowing passengers to peek out at the moving terrain.

The entertainment room merged with the vessel's glass cockpit. A large chair, bolted to thick glass and copper plating, was surrounded by levers and brakes. Each one was unfamiliar to Jocelyn, except the steering wheel. She knew how to use that. It too was as uniquely beautiful as the rest of the ship, covered with silver and laced with gold twine. What the outside lacked in appearance, the interior made up for tenfold.

Jocelyn laid her bags next to the other luggage. Her reflection in a porthole stopped her. Gasping, she shifted away from the image. The bruising from her nose bled under her eyes, shading them in dark purples and blues. Her auburn hair, now black as night, was cut to her shoulders, unevenly. She ran her hand through it. The ink would wash out, but it would take months for it to be gone completely. Jocelyn swallowed the sadness creeping up. She lost parts of herself everywhere she went, and there was more to be lost.

Benlar heaved the chest onto the ship.

You weren't expecting this, were you? I wasn't when I unloaded those. He nodded at the neatly stacked baggage and trunks.

It's pretty. But I still don't think it's going to last long. Did you see the outside? It's falling apart.

Piean swam into the water vessel, sliding her luggage under one of the six chairs.

It has made it this long. It's not going to die anytime soon. Piean patted the side of the ship and slid into the driver's seat.

Laza locked the door behind him. *Get comfortable. We are going to be in here for a long time.* He sat at the table.

The vehicle rumbled to life, shaking the octopus chandelier. Piean pushed a lever, and the machine creaked forward. *Where are we heading?* Piean asked.

To the Atlantic, then north, Laza said.

Piean nodded, pushing the lever down farther, giving the water vessel more energy to move faster.

We're heading toward Thessa? Panic escaped Benlar's voice.

Yes, but we are not going there, but around, Laza answered.

A map formed in Jocelyn's mind. North of Thessa was her homeland, and farther up was where she'd changed into a human and washed onto the shores of Ireland. Her grandmother, Avia, had brought her there, searching for Helo. They were to stay on land until he came for them. Avia was close! Jocelyn prayed her grandmother had found him.

"What do you mean there's something wrong with them?" the merchant asked, peering into a cage of white hens.

"They're sickly. See? One died," Thomas said.

Thomas pointed to a dead chicken surrounded by the clucking birds. Last night he'd ordered his manservant, Mr. Marklee, to snap its neck.

A cow mooed from the open field. The merchant's farm danced with free-range animals. His little bungalow rested on top of the hill, overlooking the ocean.

"We want a trade. Healthy livestock for these."

The thin merchant opened the cage and grabbed a hen. The bird flapped its wings, struggling to be free. The man flipped it upside down and held it by its scaly legs. The bird's wings spread as it went limp. He examined the animal.

"No. These birds are healthy. The dead one is your issue, not mine," the man said, stuffing the bird back in with the others.

Aidan stepped forward. The hot, humid air stuck to his skin. "We are not asking for a refund. Just a trade. You can sell these birds to the next bloke."

"Unless you wish us to tell our colleagues of this unfortunate affair," Thomas added.

The man looked from Thomas to Aidan, then back at the chickens. "Fine. But my animals are healthy."

Aidan turned to Nicholas and whispered, "Make sure the animals get on the ship."

"Aye, Captain. Where ye be off too?" Nicholas folded his arms over his chest.

"I have questions about what happened to Jocelyn before we left India, and I believe Mrs. Howard might have answers."

Aidan walked away from the group of sailors and Thomas.

Thomas galloped after him. "Do not disappear. We need to talk of final arrangements before your departure. Understand?" Thomas walked next to him.

"I'll meet you at the Horse Head Tavern after sunset. I have a few more inquiries to make before I leave."

Thomas stopped, the dust from the path clouding over his black boots. "You should learn to quiet your ghosts."

Aidan turned, walking backward. "How else am I to know the truth?"

CHAPTER 17

Anne Howard sat in a wicker chair on the porch of the club house, fanning herself with a silk fan. Her eyes were closed, her body sagged in the seat, and her pudgy legs stretched out into the pathway, uncaring of other guests.

"Mrs. Howard?" Aidan asked, walking the three steps onto the large porch. Almost a week ago, this woman had brought Jocelyn to him. He had run to her carriage to find his love dying. He fled this country because of Anne's advice to do so. And he lost Jocelyn in the process of saving her.

Anne flung forward, eyes wide. "You're back?" She peeled herself from the chair. "Is the girl all right?"

"She's on the ship," Aidan lied. She could never know the truth. "Jocelyn's resting. She looks to recover to her full health."

Anne exhaled a sigh of relief and sat back in her chair. "Thank the Lord. I've been praying for that poor child. Why are you back?"

Aidan took a seat next to her. "We had a mishap with the livestock."

"That's unfortunate."

"It's been resolved. Mrs. Howard…"

"Dear boy, call me Anne. Mrs. Howard is too formal for hot weather." Anne picked up her fan and opening it. An ocean scene was painted on the silk fabric. Gray seagulls sailed over white-tipped waves that rolled onto the sand.

"I need you to take me to the girl," Aidan said.

Anne gripped her fan. "You cannot be serious." She wiggled forward, inching toward Aidan. "What I witnessed was unnatural. I will never go back."

"Then tell me how to get there. I need to speak with the girl."

Anne shook her head. "They won't let you see her."

"Why not?"

"You are an outsider, and Damini is now a walking miracle."

Aidan took her hand. "You don't understand. I need to speak with her. I need answers about Jocelyn."

Anne patted his hand with her free one. "I don't believe you'll like what you find."

"Please," Aidan said.

Anne wrinkled her nose. "Fine."

Aidan squeezed her hand tighter. "Thank you."

"If they say you can't see her, we leave. Are we clear?"

He nodded. "Of course."

Laza gave Piean coordinates and then disappeared into the back room, where Jocelyn saw bunk beds against the wall before he shut the door behind him. For hours, the water vessel cut through the ocean, searching for a strong current to carry them toward Thessa. Jocelyn gazed out of a porthole at the moving sea world. Dolphins twirled around the ship in a playful manner, chirping to each other. She cracked open the window to listen to them. Their language was unique and beautiful. Jocelyn pushed her tongue to the roof of her mouth to mimic the frolicsome mammals' language.

A smaller dolphin peered through the window. Its dark eye stared at Jocelyn, listening. She made the sound again, and the animal chirped back. It turned onto its back and swam with the ship, watching her.

You were always good with language studies, Benlar said.

And you were always bad at it, Jocelyn teased.

She pushed her palm against the cool porthole. The dolphin flipped over and tapped his nose against the thick layer of glass separating them.

It helped that my parents were healers, she said, pulling her hand away from the window. Clicking her tongue, she sent the dolphin swimming back to its pod.

Maybe. Benlar looked at her.

Jocelyn sat on a fainting sofa pressed against the wall of the metal vessel. The burnt-orange fabric, made from baleen, was decorated with a gold starfish and seaweed print. Carved sea horses emerged from the coral frame's curved armrests. Jocelyn's gold tail hung over the edge of the settee.

Your hair looks good, Benlar said.

Jocelyn shrugged. *It doesn't feel right.* She ran her fingers through the dark strands, untangling them.

It will help, he said.

I know. It's just that everything is changing. I don't know who I am anymore.

The vehicle pulled sharply to the right. Jocelyn grabbed the edge of the sofa, steadying herself as small objects rolled on the table.

Thank God, Piean yelled from the cockpit.

Jocelyn and Benlar stared her way. Hidden by the large pilot chair, they had almost forgotten she was there. Almost.

The mermaid swam up, rolling her neck in slow circles, popping the strained joints. *That took longer than I thought.*

Benlar straightened as the girl swam into the room, her back to Jocelyn. *Couldn't find the current?*

It's hard looking for something you can't see, Piean countered, stretching her arms above her head and yawning.

Is this your first time out of Ommo? Jocelyn asked.

Piean peeked over her shoulder and spoke with a snobby accent. *Of course not. Every spring I visit my family's summer home in Thessa. Then I lollygag to my winter home...*

Not everyone from outside Ommo is wealthy, Jocelyn said, rolling her eyes.

I am, Benlar said, smiling.

Your parents are rich. Not you. Jocelyn laughed.

Oh, that's right. My dear parents. Now they are wealthy, and they do actually speak like that. Benlar mimicked Piean's snobby accent. *We own a summer, winter, spring, autumn, day, night, holiday, and whatever else house my cold heart desires,* Benlar stated, leaning against the table.

Piean sat in a chair across from him. *How many homes do they really own?* Piean asked, curiosity widening her eyes.

Benlar blushed. *I really don't know. They've lived so long, they've acquired real estate all over the world.*

How old are they? Piean asked.

Shouldn't you be driving this thing? Jocelyn asked.

It's on autopilot, and this current will carry us to Findora, Piean answered, irritation stirring in her voice from the interruption. *So how old are they?*

My father is seven hundred and fifty-eight, and my mother...

She's going to kill you for talking about her age, Jocelyn said.

She's five hundred-ish. One of our homes is next to a hibernation clinic.

Really! Piean jumped forward. *Have you ever been in hibernation?*

Done being far from the conversation, Jocelyn swam over to the table and sat next to Benlar. *No.* Jocelyn answered for him.

Once, Benlar corrected.

Shock washed over Jocelyn's face. *What!*

How old are you? Piean asked.

Yes, how old are you?

Benlar cleared his throat. *I appear nineteen, but in fact I'm nineteen and a half.*

Jocelyn smacked his shoulder.

Piean's forehead crumpled, confused.

The first year in — Benlar switched to his snobby accent — *Landwalker Academy* — then back to his normal voice — *they sent us above, to a fishing village where there was a measles outbreak. Even though I was vaccinated, it hit me hard. I was put in hibernation for a week to cure me. I was told I de-aged two or three months, but who knows.*

What did it feel like? Piean asked.

Like taking a long nap and waking up still tired. It took me a few days to feel normal.

Jocelyn took Benlar's hand. She liked being near him. He was the closest thing she had left of family.

And how old are you? Piean asked, glaring at Jocelyn.

Jocelyn shifted her stare to the mermaid. *Eighteen. Before you ask, I've never been in hibernation.*

You could be lying, Piean said. She quickly turned to Benlar. *If you are wondering, I'm seventeen.*

Jocelyn tightened her jaw. She wanted to reach over and pull this girl's long, natural-colored hair. But she didn't. She sat there staring, tightening her hold on Benlar's hand.

Piean shifted in her chair, the freak of nature's glare making her nervous. *With the reward on your head, I would imagine you come from a very powerful family. And with power comes wealth.*

Jocelyn's shoulders dropped. *We had what we needed, but we weren't wealthy. My mother, father, and grandmother were healers, my grandfather a teacher of mechanics. He taught at the university. That's why we lived in Savmoro. But that didn't make our family anything important.*

Benlar brushed his thumb over the top of Jocelyn's hand, encouraging her to speak more.

I've never been outside of Savmoro. There was no need to leave. The university was a few blocks from where we lived, and my parents taught me from home. I don't think I ever traveled farther than a few miles from our house. There was a coral reef behind the university, one of the most beautiful places I know of. The temperature of the water in the ship dropped as Jocelyn exhaled, unsure she wanted to say the words out loud. *My mother died there. Fiar slit her throat, and she bled all over the yellow coral. He killed my father too.*

Piean sat back in her chair. The hatred in her heart faded a little. *I'm sorry.*

Jocelyn lifted her hand from Benlar's, staring at the copper octopus above them. *Did you see it?*

Benlar shook his head. *We weren't there.*

Piean shifted her eyes between the two.

Benlar continued. *Your father was killed in the heart of Thessa. They wanted to show what would happen to anyone who crossed the city. My grandmother said they drove a spear through his heart after cutting the fin from his tail.*

Jocelyn closed her eyes, and memories festered. Her

mother and father held her five-year-old hands tight. *You will always be ours,* their loving voices repeated from the past.

What did he do? Piean asked, bringing Jocelyn back to the reading room.

I don't know. But I have a feeling they were trying to save me, she answered.

Benlar's arm reached over and pulled her to him. Jocelyn couldn't stop the pain from erupting. Her chest heaved as she struggled to breathe between sobs.

I never knew my parents, Piean said.

Mine are junicoms, Benlar added.

Jocelyn rested her head against his chest. *Mine were perfect.*

CHAPTER 18

The muscles in her neck stretched to accommodate her sleeping arrangement. Her head rested on Benlar's chest. His fingers played with her dark hair. The ship's soft rumble rocked her, keeping her in the daze a little longer. Clearing her throat, Jocelyn opened a heavy eyelid. The lit chandelier cast a warm glow over the room, and the flames shimmered through the water onto the wall.

Laza sat at the table, his head held up by his resting arm. His other hand wrote in a journal.

Where are we? Jocelyn asked.

She rubbed her stiff neck, sitting straight on the fainting chair.

Benlar smiled at her. His arm lay behind her on the sofa's frame. He flicked the porthole's lock with his finger.

Findora, Laza said, glancing at her.

Jocelyn peered out the window. *How long have I been asleep?*

A dim streetlamp passed. Then another and another. Their light washed over white sand and other moving submarines.

Four hours, Benlar said, kicking away from the chair.

I told him to put you in a berth, but he said he was fine. Laza closed his journal.

I am fine, Benlar stated.

I slept on you the whole time? Jocelyn asked.

It's not like I had anything else going on, Benlar said.

Piean poked her head around the pilot's chair. *We need to refuel.* She spotted Jocelyn on the couch. They stared at each other for a moment. *Did you sleep well?* Piean's tongue held back any witty remarks.

Jocelyn liked the mean Piean more than this one. The pity in her eyes made Jocelyn look away and peer at the rug's frayed edges. *I should've never told her,* Jocelyn thought to herself. *Where are we stopping?* Jocelyn asked.

Any grocer will have CNG, Benlar said.

Laza swam to the porthole on the other side of the vessel. *The convenience of living in a large city. The mine was the only place we could get compressed natural gas. No need to carry it elsewhere; no one would have bought it.*

Not a lot of merpeople have a water vessel in Ommo? Jocelyn asked.

Only a handful, including me. No need to. Very few travel outside of Ommo, Laza said, peering at the tall buildings surrounding them. *When we stop, you need to hide in the back.*

Jocelyn opened her mouth to protest but stopped. If she left this ship, she wasn't only putting her life at risk, but their lives also.

I see one, Piean said.

Benlar swam over to Jocelyn. *Do you want anything?*

She shook her head.

Go hide, Benlar said, kissing her forehead.

Jocelyn swam toward the door surrounded by trunks and luggage. The large mirror held her reflection as she passed it. She glanced at herself. Piean's green seaweed shirt hugged her body.

Clothes, Jocelyn said, turning to look at Benlar. *I need clothes.*

You can borrow some of mine, Piean called over her shoulder.

I would like my own, Jocelyn said.

Benlar nodded. *I'll see what I can do.*

Aidan held tight to the basket filled to the brim with fresh fruit and wrapped meats. The carriage bounced up the dirt road on a steep hill. His teeth rattled in his head.

"How much farther?" he asked, pulling out a pocket watch.

Sunset was in a few hours. Anne took longer than expected getting ready to see the villagers. For hours, Aidan had paced the porch of her home. But when she emerged, Anne was a different woman. Her white dress had been changed out for a blue one and a matching hat with fabric flowers lining the band. "This is their favorite," Anne had said, handing him the basket.

He tapped his foot, ready to jump out of the carriage and run up the hill.

"Don't be impatient," Anne scolded.

"I'm not. I have to meet my employer at sunset."

"You might be late."

The carriage slowed to a stop. Makeshift huts covered the green field, and cloth doors flapped with the slow breeze from the forest. The smell of dirt and tropical flowers settled over Aidan. He inhaled deeply. Monkeys called to each other from the treetops. There was peace in this place.

Villagers emerged from their homes, studying Aidan as he

stepped out of the buggy. Woman and children hid behind huts as men frowned and raised their chests to let him know he wasn't welcome.

"Mr. Boyd."

He turned to find a gloved hand reaching out from the carriage.

"Would you mind?" Anne asked.

"Of course not." Aidan put the basket on the red dirt, then took her hand and helped her out of the horse-drawn vehicle.

Faces lit up with Anne's appearance. Children ran from behind their homes, shouting her name.

"My dear little ones!" Anne called out to them.

Small hands pushed past Aidan to get to her. The children rubbed her skirt between their fingers. The melody of murmured "ohs" and "ahs" escaped their mouths.

A little girl, no older than three, pointed to Anne's head. "Topee. Topee. Topee," the little girl repeated.

Anne pulled out a long sapphire-jeweled hatpin, took off the hat, and handed it to the child. The girl put it on her head and covered her eyes, laughing. All the kids joined her, taking turns with the hat.

"Kahaan hai Damini tatha Raahi?" Anne asked slowly in Hindi.

The children pointed to the hut in the center of the village.

Anne smiled down at the children. "Grab the basket, Mr. Boyd."

Aidan lifted the load and held it at his side.

Anne patted the children's heads as she walked through the group. A boy pulled the tips of her glove. "Dastaana?" he asked.

"These too?" Anne giggled, slipping her hands from the gloves and handing them to the boy. "Mr. Howard is just going to have to take me shopping again." She gave the boy a big hug before continuing on.

"Is this where you took Jocelyn?" Aidan asked, slowing his steps to match Anne's.

She nodded. "Do you speak Hindi?"

"Very little."

"They speak very little English."

"Can you translate for me?" Aidan asked.

Anne glanced up at the captain. "To tell you the truth, Mr. Boyd, I'm rather curious what you're going to ask. But I'm more intrigued by Damini's answer." Their shoes pattered against the fine dirt path, leaving a trail of footprints the kids followed. "What I witnessed should've never happened. Have you heard of a sin-eater, Mr. Boyd?"

"Jocelyn is not a sin-eater," Aidan answered.

"Of course not! But your Jocelyn inhaled whatever was in Damini, just as a sin-eater is rumored to inhale one's sins. Consuming it." Anne stopped walking and grabbed Aidan's arm. "Whatever she is, she's not from this world."

Aidan's heart skipped. "She's from Ireland."

Anne chuckled. "Are you sure?" She took the basket from him and walked to the door's flap. "Damini? Raahi?" Anne called out.

Raahi stuck his head out of the doorway. His sunken cheeks lifted into a bright smile when he saw Anne. He ran out of the house and hugged the woman. "Anne!"

Damini followed, wrapping her arms around her father and Anne.

Aidan stood for a moment. Not sure when to interrupt, he tapped his foot to remind Anne he was there. But it didn't help.

Aidan leaned toward Anne. "Could you ask her what happened?"

Still embracing, Anne spoke in Hindi to Damini, each word slowly pronounced.

The girl looked up at Aidan, her eyes a dark, dark brown. She spoke to him, but he couldn't understand. Anne withdrew from the two, her face white as she listened. Damini shifted her stare to Anne, finishing.

"I don't believe I heard that correctly," Anne said before speaking to Damini in Hindi.

The girl repeated herself, but slower.

"She says her mother was from the sea. She was supposed to return, but fell in love with Damini's father, Raahi. She chose to stay on land and become his wife. Her people were furious and came for her, but the villagers fought them off. Her people left, but they threatened she would not survive out of the ocean."

The girl nodded to her father. He stared at her for a long moment before going into their home.

"What happened to her mother?" Aidan asked.

Anne repeated the question.

The girl took a step toward Aidan. Hits of womanhood accented the girl's body, but her height remained that of a child's. She spoke again. Anne followed her, listening.

"Her mother died when she was seven, but she gave Damini a gift. Told her it was part of her," Anne translated.

Raahi ran out of the house and handed something to Damini.

The girl took Aidan's hand, opened his palm, and placed something small in it. She spoke again, and Anne translated. "My mother taught me to mind-speak, just like the lady did. The woman from the sea."

Aidan looked at a medallion in his hand, a yellow coral wrapped in copper wires with gears in the center. It reminded him of the one he'd bought as a present for Jocelyn in Bantry, Ireland, from Mrs. Donnell.

"Matsyaangana," the girl said.

Anne shook her head and shrugged. "I don't know what that means."

Damini pointed to the trinket in Aidan's hand. "Matsyaangana."

"It means mermaid," Aidan said.

CHAPTER 19

The sun faded into the dark horizon, leaving behind a purple sky with streaks of pink blushing the fluffy clouds. Aidan stepped out of the carriage in front of the Horse Head Tavern. The inside of the buggy darkened with the dwindling light, casting Anne in shadows as she stared at him.

"Thank you," he said.

"What are you going to do now?" she asked.

Aidan shrugged. Busy people crowded the street, pushing past him, their feet tapping on the cobblestone road. "Head back to sea."

Anne scooted closer to the door. "I feel left in the dark, Mr. Boyd. Did you find what you were looking for?"

The horse pulling the carriage neighed and scraped a hoof in the dirt as another stallion trotted by, carrying a gentleman wearing a tricorne hat.

Aidan scratched the back of his neck. "I did."

"I'm glad. I hope today will help Miss Jocelyn."

Aidan smiled at Mrs. Howard. "Thank you again."

He bowed and closed the small carriage door, patting it twice to let the driver know the conversation was finished and he could leave. He turned to walk into the inn.

"Mr. Boyd," Anne's voice called.

He spun around to see Anne's head poking out of the buggy's window.

"If she is what Damini says, then what other creatures exist in this world?" The fear in Anne's eyes pleaded for a happy answer.

He stepped toward the carriage and took the woman's hand. "I don't know."

"Is she still on your ship?" Anne asked, but by her tone, she already knew the answer.

Aidan shook his head.

Anne leaned out of the buggy and whispered in his ear. "Then I'm glad she's a mermaid."

Aidan grinned. He'd liked Anne from the first encounter in Taylor's Emporium.

She squeezed his hand. "I hope you see her again," she said, letting go of Aidan's hand. "Driver, we can go."

The buggy pushed off, crushing the dirt beneath its wheels.

"Me too," Aidan said under his breath, before turning and entering the inn.

The room was crammed with people, shoulder to shoulder. Aidan pushed through the crowd, searching for Thomas. He spotted his navy-blue hat. He was sitting at a table. Squeezing through, he made his way to the table.

Thomas's back was to the crowd. He stared out the Georgian window at the bustling street.

Aidan sat in the empty chair next to him. The small room boomed with voices.

"I ordered," Thomas said, pushing a pint of ale to Aidan.

"Thank you," Aidan said.

"I see Mrs. Howard is well."

"She is. Shall we talk business?"

Thomas took a drink of his porter.

"What do you propose for ways of communication?" Aidan asked in a hushed voice.

"I'll send a penny post to a bawdy house in Bristol every six months," Thomas whispered. "Why were you meeting her?"

Aidan titled his head. "Who?"

"Mrs. Howard. Why did you see her?"

A young man placed two plates of curry on their table. Aidan's stomach growled with delight at the spicy aroma rising with the food's steam.

"We spoke of what occurred when Jocelyn fell ill."

"You didn't tell her Miss Jocelyn is gone?"

"Of course not," Aidan lied, looking over her shoulder for anyone listening in on their conversation. But the room was filled with drunk sailors and merchants, preoccupied with themselves.

He took a drink of the ale as Thomas studied his face.

"Good. We stick with the plan. When you set sail, she will disappear with you and the ship." Thomas centered his plate in front of him, then closed his eyes and inhaled. "Eat up, Mr. Boyd. This might be the last good meal you'll have in a very long time."

Aidan shoveled the rice and deer curry onto his fork and took a bite. Garlic and green chilies heated his tongue as he chewed. Everything about this dish was wonderful. He took another bite and chewed slower, savoring the taste. Part of him wished he wasn't eating this delicious dinner so he wouldn't miss it later.

"Where do you plan to sail first? It will help if I know where you are to plan arrangements for our business," Thomas said.

Aidan ran his tongue over his teeth, collecting leftover herbs and pepper. "Back to the Atlantic. Then north."

"Toward England?" Thomas asked, shocked.

"No."

"Then where?"

"Until arrangements are made and profit is coming in, I need to keep my crew in waters we know better than any other men. With places we can disappear."

"You are captain."

Aidan took another bite. He had no intentions of sailing to England until it was necessary to collect his instructions from Thomas. But if he was to find Jocelyn, he would start at the beginning. He planned to sail back to Bantry, Ireland, where she had washed ashore so many months ago.

"Whom should I address letters to?" Thomas asked.

"James."

"An acquaintance?"

"My grandfather."

"There are good many James," Thomas said, irritated.

Aidan glanced around the room, his gaze stopping on the hook latch holding the glass window shut. His grandfather was a brilliant, gentle man according to his mother. He loved the written word and insisted his daughter learn to read. This man was the reason Aidan wasn't illiterate.

"James Ainsley," Aidan answered. His stomach flipped, ashamed for disgracing his grandfather's name in piracy.

Thomas scrunched his nose. "I once knew an Ainsley. The fat arse smelled of pig lard and coal. It will make it easy to remember to whom to address the letters, but I do hope you choose another name while at sea."

Aidan's chest rose and fell as the urge to shove Thomas from his chair intensified with every word ridiculing his grandfather's name. "Why is that?" he asked through a clenched jaw.

Thomas's hazel eyes found Aidan's. "Because you want to be feared, not mocked. Your name should cast a shadow, bringing the brave to their knees before they ever see your face. And Ainsley will never succeed at giving such terror."

Jocelyn flicked the edge of the seaweed curtain. Brass rings secured the ocean-made material to a rod bolted to the wall, allowing privacy while sleeping. The bunk beds were long but shallow. Two covered both sides, allowing for sleeping quarters. With the drapery closed, Jocelyn felt trapped.

The hinges of the water vessel moaned as it opened. Jocelyn froze, her eyes glued to the door. She knew it had to be one of her companions, but her heart raced with the thought of it being someone else.

Mli? Benlar's voice called.

Jocelyn breathed out her held breath, relief washing over her. *I'm back here,* she said, swimming out of her bunk.

She opened the door to find Benlar and Piean removing items from a basket onto the table—jars of food, methane clathrate, and clothes.

Jocelyn picked up a dark leather corset and held it up. Silver rings lined the bottom. *Is this for me?*

There's three. It's all they had, Benlar said.

Jocelyn lifted another.

The front fastened with brass hooks and eyes to flaps of underwater-treated leather that arrowed up to the collar of the corset. Sewn-in pockets cornered the bottom. A black nylon material covered the sides where gills would be.

No seaweed or baleen? Jocelyn asked.

What's the matter? You don't like them? Piean asked, smiling as she pulled a book from the bag.

No, it's just very revealing, Jocelyn said, used to shirts that covered most of her chest.

Here, Benlar tossed a white shirt at Jocelyn. *I figured you might need this.*

Thank you! Jocelyn said, excited to spare her modesty.

Benlar pulled out an oversized leather vest with a white undershirt. Since he'd left his belongings in his room in Ommo, he only possessed the shirt on his back, the weapons he'd packed, and the money he'd taken back from Piean.

Laza swam in last, carrying a handful of waterproof paper. *Did you refuel?* he asked Piean.

Of course. Piean rolled her eyes.

Laza spotted the book on the table. *How much did that cost you?*

Piean crossed her arms. *Don't worry, it wasn't your money.*

I know, dear. Books are not cheap, and if you must spend your money on one, why buy that rubbish?

Because I like them, Piean countered.

Jocelyn glanced at the title. *Dance with Death.* With the cost of waterproof paper and the thickness of the book, she figured Piean spent a lot of someone else's money on the work of fiction.

Have you read it? Piean asked.

Jocelyn shook her head.

Piean pushed it across the table. *Give it a try.*

What about you? Jocelyn asked, looking at the book more closely. The cover had a merwoman aiming a crossbow at a merman doing the same.

Don't worry. I got two. Piean pulled out another book. *We'll switch when we're done.*

Thank you.

Jocelyn nervously took the book from the girl who'd broken her nose only a few days ago. But they had a long trip ahead, and reading sounded much better than talking.

We need to get going, Benlar said, pulling his worn shirt over his head.

Piean and Jocelyn both stared at his bare chest. Benlar swung the undershirt over his shoulders and buttoned it. For a quick second, his eyes met Piean's. She fumbled her book, dropping it on the table.

I saw posters of Mli tagged on the bulletins. It's not safe here, he added.

Piean nodded, lifting her book and pressing it to her. *I'll warm up the ship.*

CHAPTER 20

In the tiny bathroom, Jocelyn slipped the white shirt over her head and folded the cuff to her elbows. It fit well. She peered at the mirror. Her dark hair curved under her chin, making her look paler. Her nose was twice the normal size, and both eyes were bruised. She glanced at the shirt. On land she wore beautiful dresses made of silk and cotton. This was stiff and boring.

Lifting one of the corsets she had brought in with her, she admired the design. She wrapped it around the white shirt and fastened the hooks and eyes in place. Her spine was forced to straighten with the thick leather. Running her fingers down the boning, she looked into the mirror, and a merwoman stared back.

Jocelyn exhaled. For a moment she had controlled the ocean and had been powerful. Strong.

She braided the sides of her hair and tied the ends together. Opening the door, she swam out of the bathroom and into the sleeping quarters.

Piean lay on a top bunk, flipping through her new book. The mermaid glanced at Jocelyn as she swam by. *It doesn't look bad*, Piean said, then went back to reading.

Jocelyn pulled at the corset. *Is that a compliment?*

Yep.

Who's driving this thing? Jocelyn asked.

Benlar. Piean turned on her side, her head resting on her hand, and held her place in her book with her thumb. *I'm sorry about your parents. I didn't know.*

A knot formed in Jocelyn's throat. It hurt to swallow. *Thank you.*

Laza's a good merman. He'll take care of you, Piean said.

Jocelyn leaned against the frame of stacked beds. *How did he know I would come to Ommo? I mean, the sea is huge.*

No one knew where you were going to reappear. He was told to look for you. The way I understand it, he wasn't the only one. Whoever your grandfather is, he's important. There are a lot of merrows working for him, and whatever you are — Piean searched for the right words — *you're going to change things.*

Jocelyn studied Piean's pretty face. The anger in the girl's eyes was gone, they even seemed approachable, but Jocelyn's gut turned with the idea of trusting her. *What does he know about me?*

Piean shrugged. *I didn't know you existed until six months ago. That's when Laza handed me a picture of you. When I asked who you were, he told me you were someone special, and we needed to make sure no one else found you. He told me to search, and I did. A boy saw you fall from above. He knew I was looking for an outsider. I paid the little brat five gold coins for your location, and I don't think I was the only one.*

Jocelyn swam to the top bunk across from Piean and sat. *When you found me...*

I didn't know what you could do, but I knew who you were.

Why didn't you just tell me?

Piean shook her head. *There was no way you were going to trust me.*

How do you know? Jocelyn asked, irritated.

Piean looked at her book, memorized the page number, closed it, put it on the mattress, and sat up. The two girls stared at each other, their tails flicking inches from each other's.

You lied about your name, Piean stated.

You broke my nose!

And I'm sorry about that, but if you swam off, someone else would've seen you.

So you hit me in the face?

Well, you didn't swim off.

Jocelyn gaped at Piean for a long moment before bursting into laughter. *No, I didn't.*

Piean leaned closer to Jocelyn. *What does it feel like?*

My nose breaking? Jocelyn asked, her voice rising from the surprised question.

Piean shook her head. *No. To do what you do?*

Gripping the metal rail, Jocelyn lay back on the bed, her gold tail hanging off the edge. *Like falling.*

I don't understand, Piean said.

Jocelyn raised her arms and released her control over them. *Here you simply drift to the ground as the ocean embraces you.* Her limbs sank slowly to her side. *But above, when you fall, your heart races and everything becomes a blur, other than what's right in front of you. For a moment, it feels as if you're flying. Then you hit hard.* Jocelyn sat up and pushed herself off the bed. *It's terrifying that something so beautiful can cause so much pain.*

She pushed open the door that led to the parlor.

Before I die, I would like to fall, Piean said, lifting her book, then laying it back down.

It will change you, Jocelyn said, closing the door behind her.

After leaving Horse Head Tavern, Aidan recovered his laundry from a local washerwoman's home—thankful she hadn't sold them off for profit. He heaved the sack over his shoulder and strolled toward the beach, heading for the rowboats. By now the livestock and supplies should have been loaded onto the ship. And with Nicholas in charge, Aidan hadn't worried about it not getting done.

The full moon cast a silver hue over the waters, blending the sky and ocean into one. The susurrus of the waves brought serenity. Aidan spotted his former first mate and waved. Gregory sat in the last rowboat remaining on the beach, buttoning and unbuttoning his vest—waiting. The man's face pale. He jumped up and ran to Aidan.

"Someone told!" Gregory yelled, his foot catching on a loose rock. His arms flailed as he regained his balance.

Aidan's stomach dropped. He ran to close the distance between him and Gregory. "Who?"

"I don't know, but I overheard that the authorities are on their way. You need to leave!"

The men ran to the boat. Aidan threw in the bag of clothes and pushed his shoulder against the craft, the toes of his shoes digging in the sand.

Gregory joined him. The sand scraped against the bottom of the vessel. Water lapped over their boots, soaking through the worn leather.

"Get in!" Gregory yelled.

Aidan leaped into the rowboat and grabbed the oars. He speared the sharp edge of the paddle into the shallow water. "Come on," Aidan said, waving his friend onto the ship.

His friend shook his head as the ocean waves hit his thighs. "I can't."

"If you stay…"

"I will take my chances," Gregory interrupted.

"Don't be a fool. Get in!"

The pull of the tide grabbed the boat, putting strain on the wood oar.

"I can't be a pirate, not even with you as captain. You need to leave. Mr. Corwin is already aboard, and I fear he will not wait for you."

"Thomas?"

"Whoever turned you in knew your arrangements. He accused Mr. Corwin of insurance fraud," Gregory said.

A wave hit the boat, sending it into Gregory's chest. The man fell into the water but kept his head above.

Voices echoed, and lights flickered in the tree line.

"Go!" Gregory yelled, pushing the boat out to sea.

Aidan feathered the oar and rowed, leaving his friend behind. His breathing shook his body. He would be hunted. The peaceful arrangement with Thomas ruined. Aidan's shoulders heaved the weight of the ocean as he pushed his vessel toward his ship. His eyes stayed locked on Gregory. The man shoved his way out of the water and ran toward the men emerging from the forest, his hands raised in the air.

"I tried to stop him!" Gregory screamed at the top of his lungs.

Gunfire cracked in the distance.

Aidan struggled to breathe as Gregory fell to his knees, then to his chest, his face buried in the sand.

The world stopped. Aidan blinked. He tried to focus on the distant rumble of waves. Another gunshot brought him back to the situation at hand. Men in red uniforms marched into the ocean, pointing their rifles at him.

Shivers ran down his spine. Aidan sank the oars into the ocean and heaved, racing across the surface. His muscles burned with each row, but it was a dull ache compared to the pain in his frozen heart. He focused on the lifeless body of Gregory, growing smaller with each pull of the paddles. His friend was dead because of Aidan's desire to stay at sea. Because he wanted to find Jocelyn. The bitter ocean splashed onto his neck as the blade of the oars sliced through the water.

A cloud of smoke fogged the distant shore. Aidan focused on the red flashes of igniting gunpowder. A shadow slid over the small boat, engulfing him in darkness. He steered the boat to the stern of his ship. Aidan pulled the oars from the water and laid them at the bottom of the rowboat.

Two thick ropes dropped from the top deck of the large ship. Aidan looped one through a hole at the bow of the watercraft and tied a bowline knot. He rushed to the other side, tying the second rope to the vessel.

The hawser tightened, lifting the watercraft from the dark waters, swinging the smaller vessel. Gravity pulled against him, but Aidan kept his eyes on India's shore.

If they wanted a pirate to hunt, then he would give them one.

CHAPTER 21

Aidan gazed out the dining room's large multi-paneled windows. He kept his hands folded behind his back, his legs spread shoulder-width apart, grounding himself. He watched the silhouette of Calcutta dissolve into darkness.

Thomas sat at the walnut table with his hands covering his face, quiet. The tension in the room made it hard to breathe.

The recurring image of the bullet piercing Gregory's heart and him falling into the sand repeated itself in Aidan's mind. There should have been a trial. His first mate would've been found innocent. But there was none, just a line of men with guns and the authority to shoot. And Aidan had left him.

The ache in his jaw returned him to the present. Aidan must've been clenching his teeth for hours. He opened his mouth, relieving the pressure. "How could you be so stupid?" he asked, his back to Thomas.

The chair creaked under Thomas's weight as he shifted.

"Your arrogance…"

"Do not blame me," Thomas interrupted.

Rage boiled in his heart, heating his face. Aidan spun and stomped to the table. He slammed his fist down, the wood fracturing on impact. "How dare you!" Aidan shouted.

Thomas flung his chair, standing tall. "You're the one who decided to take over this ship."

"And you are the one who told our plan to your servant," Aidan said, his lip twitching.

Thomas blinked. "Mr. Marklee..."

"Was your responsibility."

"Bloody hell." Thomas sank into the hard chair. "He's worked for my family for decades. My father trusted him. I trusted him."

Aidan straightened. "You are not your father."

"I know."

Aidan paced the room with long strides, resisting the urge to hit something or someone. Time to prepare his crew and himself was lost in India. Every man's head now had a bounty looming above.

"If you return, can you clear this situation? Tell the authorities Mr. Marklee leaked false information. Clear your name and this ship?" Aidan asked.

"Do you not wish to be a pirate anymore, Captain Ainsley?"

Aidan's dark-brown eyes glared at Thomas from across the room. "Do not toy with me, Mr. Corwin, and do not call me that."

"Do you not understand? Mr. Marklee knew everything, not just about this venture."

Aidan stopped.

"I can never return. My company is ruined. Everything I have is gone," Thomas said, sadness cracking his voice.

"You had everything. Your father made sure of that," Aidan said.

"Not everything."

"What did you do?"

Thomas inhaled. "I was one of the benefactors to Charles Stuart's cause."

Aidan grabbed the back of a chair to steady himself. "The Jacobites?"

Thomas nodded.

"How could Bonnie Price Charlie's taking the throne benefited you?"

"The trading company would've had great advantages with a king's blessings."

"You call yourself an Englishman, yet you turned on your king to gain in business. Where is your loyalty?"

"To myself." Thomas picked at splitting wood. "No one was to know. If the uprising succeeded, I would've had the future king's favor."

"But the Jacobites lost at the battle of Culloden last year."

"And I remained in good standing with King George, until now."

A burst of laughter rattled Aidan's chest. "And you allowed Mr. Marklee to be present in your treason to the crown?"

"He addressed all my letters."

The English army would stop at nothing to capture a traitor to the crowd and the pirates he accompanied. Aidan's heart thudded against his ribs as he pulled out the chair and sat. "Where was your contact?"

"Ireland."

"Your visits with your aunt were a decoy."

Thomas scratched the back of his neck. "My dear insufferable Aunt Edith. The trips were routine, making my presence on the island unquestioned. It was the perfect cover."

Aidan ran his thumb over the stubble growing on his chin. "The crown will seize all of your assets."

"I know."

"You will be executed."

"I know, but so will you and this crew. There is little tolerance for piracy."

Thomas was right. There was no turning back. Aidan locked eyes with him. "Then we do what we need to do to survive. We carry a burden of silk, teas, and spices..."

"And where are we to trade?" Thomas huffed.

"Madagascar."

Thomas tilted his head.

"We'll head for Libertalia."

"Libertalia?" Thomas repeated, surprised.

"Yes, and with the money we gain from trade, we'll buy more cannons, weapons, and supplies, and restock the ship. From there we'll head for the middle passage, and the first ship we see, we'll plunder, leaving their crew unharmed, if possible," Aidan said.

He stood and faced the window. The black water mirrored the bright moon.

"Libertalia is nothing more than a legend," Thomas declared.

"I've seen it."

"That's impossible! That pirate colony doesn't exist."

"Your father took me there."

"Absurd. My father would never turn to piracy."

"Of course not. Did you ever wonder why the Corwin Trading Company never lost a ship to a pirate?" Aidan asked.

"Luck."

"Luck is an illusion people rely on to give hope to a situation they cannot control. Your father had control over everything."

Thomas leaned forward. "He paid them off?"

"No. He built them a city."

Rattling, the propellers spun at full speed under the watercraft. The pitometer log wavered between eighty and ninety knots as they sped through the ocean, traveling alongside other vehicles heading north.

If we keep this up, we'll be in Savmoro in about ten days, Piean said, bouncing around the cockpit, pressing buttons and checking gauges.

Benlar slept on the fainting chair, his head pressed against the porthole.

Jocelyn sat at the table in the entertaining room. She picked up the book she'd borrowed from Piean and flipped through the pages. The writing was different than the books she'd read in Edith's home. The letters curved and flowed across the page, connecting together in a wave of arches and slants, making it easier to read.

Genetically transferred languages passed from parents to children. When she was old enough, her mother had brought Jocelyn to assist her with the birthing of a local merwoman who chose to have her child in the ocean instead of on land. Jocelyn hid in the corner of the room as the soon-to-be mother screamed in agony. The baby was born with two tiny legs. She stared at them—Jocelyn had never seen feet before. The child's lungs heaved as it choked on the water.

Jocelyn's mother placed the family medallion, crafted from the parents' combined bloodline, on the infant's chest. The talisman glowed, embedding itself into the skin, and within painful moments, the crying child had a blue tail. At that moment, Jocelyn knew she could never be a healer.

Morphing brought knowledge, and a child's mind absorbed the information. By age three, most children knew over fifty languages, and combined with studies, over a hundred by age six, if their parents passed on a wide array of dialects.

Jocelyn read the first line of the novel: *The world was cruel to the unwanted.* This was perfect for Piean and her everyone-is-against-me attitude. She read on as she sat at the table. The gas lanterns lit the small space, and the temperature of the water cooled as the ship headed north, deeper into the ocean, chilling the metal of the submarine.

Seated at the head of the table, journals surrounded Laza. Reading from one of them, the elderly merman curled the ends of his graying red hair around his finger.

Jocelyn glanced over at him. He shivered.

What are you reading? Jocelyn asked, putting down her book.

My old research logs.

She slid his closest journal to her and flipped open the black cover. The pages were thick, made of layers of manufactured plastic, paper, and ink. When pressure was applied, the ink stained the paper between the plastic, keeping it from washing away. Laza's sloppy scroll covered the parchment.

The two plasmas interfused. Sample M dominated over Sample H, eliminating healthy cells, resulting in death for the host, Jocelyn read to herself as she remembered his lab. Her stomach churned. She couldn't help wonder who he'd experimented on.

Laza pushed his chair toward a gothic copper stove in the corner of the room.

Is this what's in all of the trunks? Your research? she asked.

He turned a knob on the heater. The seashell glass window glowed red as fire erupted behind it.

My memory is not young, so I rely on these. Laza pointed at the open journals.

When was the last time you went into hibernation?

Over fifty years ago. I didn't choose to be this old for fun. With my research, I never had time to spare, figuring the option would be there forever. But now it's gone. Thessa removed my funding and threw me out when they closed the studies on genetics. I lost all my privileges. Your grandfather found me before he disappeared. He placed me in the lab in Ommo and told me to do what I do best. All of my findings on bloodlines and genetics are in those trunks.

What did you find?

Laza sat, folding his hands in front of him. *All bloodlines lead to one. It's minute, but it's there.*

Do you believe it to be the mage's? Jocelyn turned the page of the journal.

No, Laza said, leaning over and grabbing the journal in front of Jocelyn. He flipped the pages to an illustration of a medallion and set the book in front of her. He tapped the page. *I believe it's the child's, and it is passed to each of us through this.*

Jocelyn ran her finger over the dyed paper, leaving a faint line. *How can that be?*

I don't know. But all of our DNA is human, except a mutant gene. That bloodline is not from this world. We would have to be supplied it at birth and hibernation. I believe that is how we are merrows.

There are more of us than ever. How can Thessa keep a vast supply for our civilization? Are they manufacturing it? Jocelyn stared at Laza.

The lineage is pure. Not fabricated or diluted. In order for them to produce enough for the population, whoever the host is must still be alive.

Jocelyn bit her bottom lip, peeling away a layer of flaking skin. *Inam is the oldest Descendent. Do you believe it could be him?*

Laza smiled as he lifted another journal and flipped it open.

He swam back and sat in his seat. The heat from the stove touched Jocelyn's face with the gentle sway of the moving water.

Maybe. No one knows how old he is. But I do wonder. In order for that much blood to be collected, whoever it belongs to must be in a lab all the time, and Inam likes to make his presence known.

What do you mean? Jocelyn asked.

Laza focused on the page of the open book, looking away from her. *There are a lot of us, and that is a lot of blood. The only way it can work, without killing the host, is if they were living in a hibernation chamber.*

Chapter 22

Hiding in the sleeping quarters became second nature whenever the submarine slowed to refuel. Jocelyn slid under the heavy blanket, reading. The hero's story of fistfights won was a refreshing change from the dull, recycled conversations among the four.

The outskirt towns faded together as days passed in a slow, mindless lull. They steered clear of Thessa. Even from a distance, the huge city was impressive. For miles, buildings spread over the dark ocean floor. At its heart was the Cathedral—home of the Descendants.

The vast building was tiered with white stones, glowing from the over-lit city. Over thirty peeked domes decorated the massive fifty-story structure. A train system ran through the building's base before curving throughout Thessa. Giant statues of the Descendants circled the Cathedral, keeping their eyes on the city and all who dared cross them.

Jocelyn had watched from a porthole as the city faded behind them and other commuting submarines faded into black specks. The gleam from the Cathedral could be seen for two days.

The walls of the vehicle were closing in with each mile, and

Jocelyn's skin crawled with the thought of being stuck inside the submarine for much longer.

Benlar paced the reading room, swimming from one side to the next. Jocelyn watched him from a bottom bunk in the sleeping quarters, her book opened in front of her. He never could sit still. She focused on the pages, flipping to the next one.

Benlar swam out of her view, his silver fin piercing through the water.

It's Savmoro! Benlar yelled.

Jocelyn slipped from the covers in a mad rush, kicking the book. It drifted to the ceiling. She swam above Laza, who was eating at the dining table, toward the cockpit.

Piean slowed the vehicle to an acceptable speed. The glass dome gave a clear view of Jocelyn's hometown as they drove thirty feet above the multicolored coral reef. Sea turtles swam alongside the watercraft.

Benlar floated near Piean. Piean glanced at him, then the control panel. Jocelyn noticed a shy smile spread across the girl's lips. Jocelyn's cheeks heated. She had looked at Aidan the same way.

The pull to be with him still tugged at her heart. She studied the wrinkles around Benlar's knuckles. Guilt rushed over her. He should be happy, but not with Jocelyn claiming him as her own.

The days confined together had lent time to talking and reading. And Piean could talk. They exchanged views on books, clothes, weapons, money, life, and the beauty of Thessa from afar.

With every passing hour, Jocelyn disliked the girl a little less. But every time Benlar got near Piean, anger bubbled up. But it wasn't for Piean, it was for herself.

Holding tight to Piean's seat, Jocelyn leaned over the driver's shoulder. Her eyes locked on the direction of her house. She wondered if her room was untouched and safe or torn to pieces. *Are we going to stop?* she asked.

Less than a year had passed since she was safe in her home —when her world was small. But life had changed, and Savmoro was no longer her oasis, but the dwelling of her nightmares.

No, Laza answered from the other room.

Jocelyn crossed her arms. *Good. No one's home anyway*, she said, swimming out of the stuffy cockpit, leaving Benlar and Piean. *How much longer?* she asked Laza. The idea of spending another day crammed between the submarine's walls flipped her stomach.

She sat on the fainting chair as her once-quiet town passed by. Merrows swam above, most making their way toward the University. The gothic building pointed toward the surface like a beacon for whoever sought enlightenment.

Jocelyn outlined the top steeple on the dirty window. They moved away from the school, leaving the drawing to drift over the fleeting town.

Not long, Laza answered.

She tapped her fingers on the window ledge. The heated water suffocated her. *How long?* Jocelyn asked.

Less than a day. Laza's calm voice slid under Jocelyn's skin.

Benlar swam over to her, lifted her tail, and slid under it, sitting on the chair. He rested her fin on his lap. The closeness burned. She sat up and moved away from him, swimming to the sleeping quarters.

Where are you going? Benlar asked.

I'm going to finish the book. Let me know when we get there.

A loud popping noise echoed from the cockpit. The three

flinched, spinning their heads toward the front of the ship.

What was that! Laza pushed himself from his seat.

A rattling noise took over, shaking the vehicle.

I don't know, but it's coming from the engine. It could be a cylinder or the transmission. I won't know until I look. Piean slowed the submarine.

Jocelyn and Benlar followed behind Laza.

We can't stop here! Benlar ordered.

It's not going to make it much farther, Piean stated, the rattling becoming louder.

There's a kelp forest a mile away. We can hide there. Jocelyn pointed to the left.

I don't think it's wise, Laza said. *We're almost there.*

We don't have a choice, unless you want to swim the rest of the way. Piean turned the wheel of the vessel and pushed on the gas, speeding away from Savmoro.

Jocelyn couldn't help but smile. Finally, she would be able to leave the stale water vessel and get fresh water—have a moment to herself.

Benlar drifted down to Jocelyn, his face inches from hers. She expected him to kiss her, but she didn't want him to.

You can't leave this ship, he said, placing his hand on her elbow.

Jocelyn's heart fell. *I've been here for nine days. We'll be hidden.*

Benlar rubbed his thumb over her skin. *I know, but we can't risk it. If they find you…*

But they won't, Jocelyn said, pulling away from him. *I'm not a child. I can make my own decisions.*

The rattling of the machine fluctuated back to a popping sound.

I know, Benlar said.

Jocelyn glared at him. *I'm going, Benlar, and I would appreciate it if you would stop trying to protect me for one second. Just give me room to breathe.*

Benlar gritted his teeth. *As you wish.* He swam away from her.

The Bay of Bengal receded as the ship's binnacle pointed southwest, sending them deeper into the Indian Ocean. Warm winds gusted, pushing against the white canvas sails.

Aidan laid his clean clothes on the feather mattress. For eight days, they'd evaded the British Navy, changing the main top castle lookout every four hours to keep fresh eyes on the horizons. The *Cliodhna's* days as a peaceful merchant ship were gone, leaving a silent, nervous crew. The men turned toward Aidan when he stepped on deck. They wanted answers he wasn't prepared to give.

Nicholas piloted the helm with the sea artist, Adam, navigating by his side. Thomas kept to his room. The lack of a manservant showed in his appearance. For the first time in his life, he was learning to dress himself.

Aidan spent hours studying the navigation charts, mapping their route to Libertalia at the north point of Madagascar. If they wanted to outrun the Navy, the vessel needed to be in perfect condition, and the ship needed to be careened before setting off for the long voyage to Europe.

If the pirate colony was safe, as he hoped it was, they would find shallow water to clean and strip the hull of barnacles and plant growth. This might be the last chance they had of maintaining the boat until they discovered another safe place to hide.

Filling the washbasin with cool water, Aidan cleaned himself then dressed. His first impression as captain would be a good one to the residents of Libertalia. He brushed his hair with Jocelyn's comb. His beard stubble had darkened with length, overtaking his chin. Aidan sat and unfolded a straight razor. He lathered soap on his face and shaved.

In less than a day, he would be introducing himself to the world as the captain of a pirate ship.

Patting dry, he stared at himself. The man looking back was unfamiliar. They had the same face, but deep in his brown eyes, he was changed. Hardened. Aidan covered his head with a leather tricorne hat and left the room.

The sun heated the galleon's planks, bleaching the wood. A warm breeze flowed over the ship as seagulls swayed with it, squawking at the men below.

Aidan made his way to the helm. Sailors rushed around him, adjusting sails to accommodate the wind.

Nicholas wiped sweat from his brow with his sleeve, his eyes squinting from the bright light. "I hear ye now be a James?" he asked as Aidan stepped closer.

Shaking his head, Aidan placed his hands on the rail and peered down at the working men. "Please don't call me that. It's a lost opportunity with what occurred in Calcutta."

"It be unfortunate what 'appened to Mr. Gregory, but ye were not blind to the possibilities."

"Do not lecture me." Aidan tapped his finger on the curved wood.

"Then stop hiding and be the captain ye promised these men."

The sea artist glanced at his captain, wide-eyed. The boldness in Nicholas brought a frown to Aidan's face.

"Please, leave us," Aidan ordered the navigator.

The short man nodded and left.

"What am I to tell them? Someone has already been killed from my selfish actions."

Nicholas flung his hand in the air. The wheel wobbled as the ocean directed the ship with its current. "Ye be nothing more than a crying child. We cannot turn back. We need a captain, and if ye cannot be 'im, then appoint another."

Aidan squeezed the rail, his knuckles white. "No one will take my ship," Aidan said through gritted teeth.

Nicholas smiled and nodded. "That be the man we need." He grabbed the wheel. "That anger is the only way we'll survive. I suggest ye leave Mr. Boyd behind and let Captain James take charge."

"I am afraid of who he will become," Aidan said, loosening his grip.

"Good," Nicholas responded.

George emerged from the belly of the ship, ran the length of the lower deck, and leaped onto the netting. He climbed the main mast, his turn to keep watch. The boy stopped, holding on with one hand, and tilted out and locked eyes with Aidan.

When Aidan gave the lad a slow nod, the boy lit up. His smile filled his face as he scurried to the top with no fear.

Nicholas yawned.

"You need sleep." Aidan grabbed the helm. "I'll take over. Tomorrow we will need everyone clear."

"Yes, Captain."

Nicholas let go of the wheel, moving out of the way as Aidan took the pegs with both hands. "How should the men address ye?" Nicholas asked.

Aidan glanced at him. "As Captain."

CHAPTER 23

Cold water rushed into the water vessel, nipping Jocelyn's nose. Long kelp stems curled into the open door. The plant grazed her arm, welcoming her home.

Benlar swam out first and disappeared into the forest, his hand over his armed crossbow, as the engine's rattling quieted away. Piean darted out second, her crossbow tucked under her arm. Jocelyn swam toward the front of the ship, stopping in the doorway. She swayed her hand through the freezing water, feeling freedom.

Cold? Laza asked, pulling on a dark-blue seaweed coat before swimming to her side and poking his head out.

Nothing I won't get used to, Jocelyn answered.

Clear, Benlar said, pushing through the thick plants. He folded his crossbow and strapped it to his belt.

Piean, let me know if you need me. I'm staying in. These waters are too cold for my liking, Laza said. The old merman turned from the doorway and went back inside, leaving the three of them alone.

Jocelyn swam out of the vehicle, her body stiff from being cooped up in a small space. Stretching her arms, she reached for the tips of the playful kelp, moving upward.

Benlar grabbed her tail, pulling her down to him. *Don't leave the forest,* he ordered.

Glancing toward heaven, she sank, the forest closing in on her. *Can I swim, or am I to stay in this one spot?*

Of course you can swim, but stay low. Benlar brushed her hair off her face. *I just want to keep you safe.*

Jocelyn moved away from his touch. He tightened his hand into a fist and dropped it to his side. *You need space, I understand.*

I might need more, Jocelyn said, glancing to the murky ocean floor.

A red crab crawled over a stone, pinching its claws at the intruders.

Then why did you kiss me?

Jocelyn rubbed her hands. *I don't know. It's what we used to do. I think you feel it too. We don't fit anymore. At least not like before.*

That's not how I feel. Go swim. Benlar shook his head. *You need to think about what you're saying.* His jaw tightened. *Aidan can only love you for one lifetime. I can give you eternity.*

Jocelyn grabbed his hand. *It's not Aidan who stops us.*

Then who?

Me. She lifted his hand to her lips and kissed it. *I need you more than ever, but I will not be with you when this is over.*

Benlar jerked his hand from her. *It's cruel to play with other's emotions.*

His breath quickened as Jocelyn watched him. She could feel his heart breaking along with their connection to each other. *I'm sorry,* she said simply, swimming away.

Her chest filled with regret. She shouldn't have waited so long; she should've told him in Ommo. But she didn't even know then. She kicked faster, paddling past Piean and the open hood of the submarine.

What's the matter? the girl asked.

He's all yours.

Excuse me?

Jocelyn stopped, facing Piean. *Benlar needs someone, and it's not going to be me.*

Did you snap? What are you talking about?

I just... The words froze on her tongue. Letting him go was the hardest thing she'd ever done. *I need to be alone,* Jocelyn said.

I don't think...

Piean! Jocelyn snapped.

Piean waved her hands in defeat. Her dark hair moved with the current of the forest. *Whatever you say. Just don't get hurt.*

Nothing can hurt me, Jocelyn said, pushing through the green leaves.

Benlar kicked to swim after Mli, but he stopped himself. The pain in his heart filled his chest, stabbing him. The girl he thought he would spend eternity loving had taken away his future with nothing more than words.

Grabbing his knife, he sliced through the swaying kelp, destroying the gentle plant. He wanted the world to feel his heartbreak. He wanted Mli to know how she'd torn him down. How unfair she was being. He spun to rush after her, sheathing his knife.

What the hell is the matter with Mli? Piean asked, swimming through the kelp. She spotted the destruction around Benlar.

Where did she go? Benlar asked.

That way. Piean pointed behind her. *But you might want to stay here.*

Pushing past her, Benlar swam in the direction Piean gave. *Don't tell me what to do.*

I'm not, Piean said. *Go find her.*

The sarcasm in the girl's voice stopped him. *You don't understand anything.*

Piean wrinkled her nose. *Yes, I do. That girl broke your heart, and now you want to tell her why she's wrong. Even if you* —she waved her hands in a swimming motion —*go swimming after her, she will never mend it. You are chasing the wrong girl.*

Benlar shook his head. *I love her.*

But do you?

He glared at her.

I'm not trying to make you mad. But you should think about it before rushing off to find her.

You know nothing about love, Benlar said.

You're right. I don't. But I know what it's like to have your heart broken over and over. To not be wanted. Don't go after her —give her room to breathe. Isn't that what she asked for? It's not like we're going anywhere until I fix this thing.

Benlar hit the stem of a long piece of kelp. If she wanted space, he'd give it. He swam in the opposite direction of Mli.

The farther Jocelyn swam, the harder it became to breathe. Grief took over. Finding a clearing in the middle of the forest, she sank to the sea's floor, her body shaking as she wept. Blue water carried the sun's light down to her, but it was cold and unforgiving.

Minutes faded into hours as her sadness drifted away. Jocelyn lay in the sand—motionless, black hair floating in the ocean.

Mli! Benlar's voice screamed for her.

Lifting herself, she stared in the direction she'd come. The leaves of the plant rustled.

I'm here, Jocelyn said, expecting Benlar to emerge from the lining of the forest.

But another merman burst through, one she didn't recognize. His silver breastplate held a spiraling seashell overlaid with gold and blue stone—the symbol of Thessa.

Screaming, Jocelyn sprinted up, but the guard was quick. He grabbed her waist and slammed her down, hitting her head on a stone.

The pain shot through her spine and into her fingers. The ocean's voice whispered in her ear as she breathed in. The gentle sway of the water quickened around them.

Jocelyn pushed against the merman's chest, but he was stronger. He pulled her to him and stabbed her with a needle. The drug heated her blood as it ran through her body, paralyzing her.

The ocean flattened the kelp in a mad rush, knocking Laza's vehicle onto its side as a cloud of sand covered it.

Inam wants to see you, the guard said, lifting her in his arms.

Jocelyn's limp body dangled in the merman's arm as he swam toward an oncoming watercraft. She tried to move, but nothing happened. She was completely helpless, watching the blue-painted submarine settle on the ocean floor.

Benlar and Piean raced to reach her. The doors of the waiting vehicle opened, and a guard started shooting at them. Benlar grabbed Piean, pushing her to the ground as arrows hit the bottom of Laza's submarine.

The guard carrying Jocelyn swam into his vessel. Eight mermen were crammed into the interior. Four of them swam out, ready to fight, closing the door behind them.

The hot sun melted into gray clouds, tinting the edges a fiery orange. Most of the crew had stripped their shirts hours ago as temperatures rose. The darkening sky brought relief not only from the heat, but from being exposed. Aidan's arms sagged from hours of manning the wheel.

Nicholas ascended the stairs to the upper deck. "Let me." His hand reached for the wheel.

"Are you sure?"

"There be only so much sleep one man can take. And I like this job."

"Good. It's yours, then. We will also need a quartermaster to man this crew and ship."

Nicholas shook his head. "Too much responsibility for me. 'Sides, shouldn't the crew vote?"

Aidan nodded. "As you wish. Gather the crew tomorrow."

"Aye," Nicholas said, gently turning the helm to match the compass with the bow of the ship.

"But be forewarned, I'll be nominating you."

"As ye wish, Captain."

Aidan laughed at Nicholas's wide smile.

He walked down the stairs to the deck. Once the ship was in order, Aidan hoped he and the crew would be ready for Libertalia. Though, part of him knew nothing would prepare him for what was to come.

CHAPTER 24

Piean unlatched her bow from her utility belt, arming it with an arrow. Two of Thessa's guards swam to the right, the other two to the left, circling Benlar and Piean, ready to shoot their crossbows.

Benlar raised his hands in the air. *I'm a landwalker for Thessa.*

The tallest of the group aimed high, for Benlar's head. *We have orders.*

What, to kill us? Piean asked, eyes darting from one merman to the next.

To do what we need to get Mli Pelizen to Thessa.

Piean looked at Benlar, panic washing over her face. *They're going to kill us.*

A dart whizzed through the water, striking the tall soldier in the neck. The merman's eyes rolled back. He collapsed, drifting to the sea floor.

The old merman! another yelled, pointing his weapon toward the overturned vessel.

Another dart shot through the water, missing an officer. Then another and another, firing from a safe distance.

Benlar grabbed his knife and swung at the distracted

guard. The blade slid into the merman's fin. Grinding his teeth, the officer lowered his weapon to grab the knife. Benlar rammed into him, slamming the butt of his steel flashlight into the side of the merman's head, knocking him out.

The two other soldiers directed their weapons and shot, but Benlar swam up as the arrows crossed.

Piean lifted her bow and squeezed the trigger, releasing an arrow at the officer in front of her. The merman was quick, dodging the deadly arrow, but swam right into one of Laza's sporadic darts. The merman drifted to the ground.

The last guard hid behind a rock. Benlar spotted him from above. Diving, Benlar overtook the officer and punched him. The guard raised his hands, dropping his weapon in surrender, his hands shaking. Benlar studied his opponent, who was younger than him and straight out of training.

Benlar hit harder, knocking the boy out. He laid the body against the rock. The lad would have a bad headache, but he would be alive.

Swimming, Benlar and Piean grabbed the weapons from the unconscious soldiers.

Hurry! Laza ordered, poking his head over their wrecked transportation.

Piean and Benlar threw the weapons on the ground near Laza, who collected everything.

Shoving their shoulders under the capsized watercraft, Benlar and Piean heaved. The underwater gravity gave little resistance, allowing the vehicle to shift upright, and loud crashing and shattering bellowed from within.

Hurry! Laza shouted, prying open the door and swimming in. He dropped the crossbows and knives on top of the mess.

The old merman shoved overturned trunks and furniture out of the way, clearing a path to the cockpit. Piean swam over him and strapped herself into the driver's chair. Benlar slammed the door shut and locked it.

Come on, Piean pleaded, turning over the engine with a long brass key.

The vessel grumbled before spitting out a dark cloud that seeped through the hood, covering the windshield.

Damn it! Piean shrieked, unfastening her belt.

She pushed past the two mermen, grabbing Benlar's arm on the way, swung open the door, and swam out with Benlar in tow.

Radiator? he asked.

I don't know. Turn it on, she ordered, lifting the hood and glancing over her shoulder at the unconscious guard.

Oil covered the engine block and a large glass square at the heart of the water vessel's life source. Benlar swam back inside and turned the key, sputtering the gears and wheels to life. The glass container glowed blue from the methane clathrate. Black smoke leaked from a cylinder head before a larger cloud shot out the back exhaust pipe with a *bang.*

Piean slammed her fists on the hood. *Camedia!*

From the cockpit, Benlar raised his hands in the air, questioning.

There's oil in the cylinders. I can't fix this here.

You have to! Benlar cried, turning off the engine. *They have her!*

I know!

Laza swam past Benlar, putting his hand on the windshield. *How far can we go?* Laza asked.

The engine will blow, Piean answered.

How far? he asked again.

I don't know. It all depends on how much oil is in the cylinders. Piean wiped her stained hands on a flapping piece of kelp.

There is no way we can catch up. It'll never match their speed.

Get in! Laza said, turning the key over Benlar's shoulder.

Benlar slid out of the chair, and Laza took his place. *Do you think we'll catch them?*

Piean swam into the watercraft, locking the door behind her. *We're not going to try. We can't.*

Benlar's head jerked up. *What! We have too.*

Helo will know what to do. We find him, and he'll help us get her back, Laza said, easing the vessel into a slow crawl over the kelp forest.

Broken glass slid to the ground as they ascended. The octopus lantern swung unevenly with the loss of three of its legs.

We have to go after her now! If they get to Thessa, we're never getting in, and she'll be gone.

Benlar reached for the wheel, but Laza grabbed the boy's hand and squeezed. *Touch the wheel again, and you will not have a hand. You love the girl. Good for you. But don't be an idiot. Use what they have taught you. Be smarter.* Laza shoved his hand away and pushed on the accelerator. *Helo can get us in. He can find her.*

Piean patted Benlar's shoulder. *He knows what he's doing,* she assured him.

If she dies, I blame you! Benlar shouted.

They won't hurt her. She's too valuable. The water vessel shuttered with the extra gas Laza fed her. *What you should really worry about is if she will believe the lies they're going to tell her.*

Inhale. One. Two. Three. Exhale. One. Two. Three, the guard directed. The merman who'd grabbed her sat in a chair facing

Jocelyn. He kept two fingers pressed to her wrist.

Breathing took every ounce of Jocelyn's strength, her chest heavy and unresponsive.

Are you going to intubate? another guard asked.

No, she's doing good. The guard smiled at her. *You're doing good. The drug is going to last for a long time. You need to remember to breathe.*

Jocelyn blinked, but her eyelids responded seconds later.

My name is Tonium, her guard said.

What are you doing? an armed merman asked, his bow pointed at the ground, ready for attack. *Don't tell her your name!*

She's a guest of Inam. Not a prisoner.

Don't talk to her! That's an order, the higher-ranking officer commanded.

Yes, sir, Tonium said.

Jocelyn tried to inhale, but her gills froze, unable to pass water through them. Her eyes drooped from lack of oxygen.

Breathe! Tonium ordered, but she couldn't.

The guard tilted her head, opening her mouth. Pressing a laryngoscope against her tongue, he slipped a tube down her throat, scratching her trachea. Blood floated from her open mouth.

Turn it on! Tonium yelled.

Water rushed through the tube and out her gills, trapping oxygen. Jocelyn closed her eyes, surrendering to the relief of breathing.

The guard patted her head. *You're all right. We'll be in Thessa soon. You'll be safe there,* Tonium reassured her.

Thomas stirred his spoon around and around, scraping the porcelain bowl.

"You should eat," Aidan said, finishing his dinner.

Thomas pushed the bowl off the table. The soup and glass shattered on the floor.

"Bloody hell!" Aidan yelled, scooting his chair away from the mess. "What's the matter with you?"

"Why do I care? I have nothing."

"Damn it, Thomas. Stop being a child."

"You don't understand because you've never had anything important. Your life meant nothing."

Aidan stood from the chair. "You've always been a spoiled ass. Your tantrums are not going to work on this ship. From now on, you have to find a job, or you're just dead weight."

"I'm more valuable than any of these peasants," Thomas hissed back.

"No, you're not." Aidan stepped over the spreading mess. "Clean this up."

Thomas leaned back against his chair, arms folded. "You need me more than you know, Captain."

"That is where you're wrong. You serve no purpose anymore." Aidan opened the door.

Thomas sneered. "You're changing, but you will always be a heartsick, lost dog."

"Maybe, but you are a man with no skills and no money — useless."

"I'm not useless!" Thomas yelled, standing. His chair fell back.

Aidan walked out of the room. "Prove it, or we leave you in Libertalia."

"You would never."

"We dock tomorrow," Aidan said, shutting the door.

CHAPTER 25

For hours the craft fought dying with loud bangs and hissing. The water vessel roared, jerking to a stop. Smoke burst out from under the hood. Laza coughed as burned motor oil filled the vents and seeped into the cockpit in a metallic rainbow.

A large mountain erupted from the sea floor a few miles in front of them.

This will do, Laza patted the machine.

It's blown! Piean said, opening the door, swimming out of the submarine into the dark water.

I know, but it made it this far. We're almost there.

Laza turned on a flashlight and kicked his white tail, heading north.

Benlar handed Piean extra arrows from the guards' weapons. *I hope he knows where he's going,* Benlar said, swimming after the old merman.

Piean turned and pushed herself back into the craft, grabbing the key. She picked up a flashlight from the mess on the ground and locked the vehicle before darting after the other two.

Helo said to meet at the south base of the Porinam seamount, Laza said over his shoulder, pointing at the mountain.

Benlar swam next to Laza, holding his own light aimed ahead. *When was the last you heard from him?*

Laza glanced at Benlar. *He contacted me when the girl disappeared. Before then, I figured he was lost.*

You're sure he can help us?

You don't know much about him, do you? Laza asked, his face beaming as they swam closer to the mountain and Piean caught up with them.

He's a scientist, Benlar said.

Laza nodded. *Yes, he is. There!*

The merman pointed his light at a round door at the base of the mountain, and silver sparkled.

It's like ours at home, Piean stated.

Because Helo built them both.

Laza swam ahead of the group, stopping at the silver door. The embossed emblem of a full tree with a bright star on its left crested on the metal. The old merman brushed his hand over the door, then knocked.

Piean swam next to Benlar.

I hope this works, he said.

She glanced at him. *Me too.*

Laza knocked again, the thud echoing in the water. The three waited.

No one's here! Benlar yelled at Laza as the old merman raised his hand again to knock. *She's gone because you wanted to hunt a ghost.*

Is that what you think I am? A ghost? A merman's voice asked from behind the group.

Benlar spun with his crossbow raised, ready to fire.

A young merman, holding a basket filled with groceries, swam with a young mermaid on his arm. The merwoman's hair was ash gray. *Did you find her?* the merman asked.

Laza bowed, his hands at his side, and stayed there.

No need for that. The merman waved, and Laza raised his head.

Benlar! Put that away! The young merwoman ordered.

Lowering the bow, Benlar peered at her. *Avia?*

Where is my granddaughter?

Gone, Benlar said, lifting his finger from the trigger and lowering his weapon.

What! The panic in Avia's voice washed over the group in a wave.

Is this true? The anger in Helo's voice overshadowed his wife's.

I'm so sorry, Helo, but she was captured outside of Savmoro by Thessa's guards, Laza said.

Piean pointed at the merman. *You're Helo?*

The merman nodded, dropping the basket.

You're younger than I expected, Piean added.

They'll reach Thessa by tomorrow. That gives us little time, Helo said, swimming past the group. He unlocked the silver door and swung it open. *Avia, grab your medical bag. We might need it.*

Avia darted into the tunnel. Helo glanced at Benlar and kicked his black tail, his dark hair in a long braid down his back. There were no pictures of Helo in Mli's home, and Benlar only knew him as an old merman, yet this young face looked familiar.

Are you good at driving? Helo asked.

Benlar nodded, but Piean swam in front of him.

I'm better, she declared.

Good, Helo said, swimming into the tunnel. *Come.*

The three followed Mli's grandfather through the doorway.

Move, Jocelyn ordered herself.

A plastic tube attached to a pump rested in her mouth, filtering oxygenated water into her chest. The fan of the machine swished the ocean, yet the poison continued to warm her blood. Her mind throbbed as she focused on her motionless thumb.

Move! But nothing happened.

The watercraft they traveled in was designed to blend in, appearing slow and average, but under the hood, it was nothing of the sort. The power the vehicle released put Laza's ship to shame. The three-day trip from Thessa to Savmoro took only eight hours in the undercover vehicle.

The vessel slowed. The silver glow of lights made it clear they were entering Thessa's city limits.

Focusing harder, Jocelyn demanded her thumb to move. She needed to able to escape or fight. The tip of her digit twitched. Excitement burst in her chest as she made the thumb jerk again, but she kept her face emotionless. Focusing on her index finger, it trembled under her mental strain.

A hand rested on top of her moving fingers. Tonium smiled down at her.

Seems the drug is starting to wear off, he said, turning off the machine.

Jocelyn's chest heaved, pushing the ocean through her gills without the ventilator's assistance.

Tonium looked into her eyes. *Close your eyes. I'm going to count to three, and it will be over.*

What are you going to do? Jocelyn asked, but Tonium grabbed the tube and slowly pulled on it.

Gagging, her throat closed around the tube.

Calm down, Tonium said.

He stopped moving the breathing tube, allowing Jocelyn to regain control of her breathing. Smiling, he tugged the pipe out.

Coughing spasms shook her. Tonium lifted her from the seaweed-wrapped cot and held her, patting her back. Blood clumped around her mouth before dissolving into the sea. Regaining control, Jocelyn inhaled the salt water. It scratched like sandpaper in her sore trachea.

The worst is over, Tonium tried to reassure her.

The warming sensation faded from her hand but stayed in the rest of her body. Jocelyn balled her hand into a fist. She gasped with relief when it responded. Her body was becoming hers once more, but at this speed, not soon enough.

Grabbing Tonium's wrist, Jocelyn peered up at him. Her head wobbled side to side. *Please, help me,* Jocelyn pleaded.

Tonium laid her down, gently resting her skull on a sponge pillow. *I can't,* he said, wiping her black hair from her face. *Inam just wants to talk.*

Jocelyn rolled her eyes. *You're either really good at lying or really stupid. It took eight guards and a paralyzing drug to bring me in to chat? Are you afraid of me?*

She tried to push her hands to lift herself, but they wouldn't support her. She flopped back onto the seaweed cot.

We are just supposed to bring you in, he answered, holding her wrist and taking her pulse. He avoided eye contact, staring at the floor.

Outside the window, the city sped by, street lamps blurring.

He killed my parents, and now you're bringing me to him, like this.

Tonium squeezed her hand. Jocelyn glanced up at him. A

thin, pointed nose centered his face, and auburn hair covered his ears.

I can't help you. His mind-talk was directed just to her, but he still whispered. He glanced at the mermen staring out the portholes at their home.

Then this is it, she said, closing her eyes.

A sharp jab in her shoulder shot open her eyes. Tonium slid a small needle from her skin, holding an empty syringe. He dropped it into a medical bag and buried it under the other supplies.

Just in case there is more than talking, you'll be able to help yourself, he said.

The warming from the drug dissolved into a chill as the antidote killed the paralyzing effect. Jocelyn gave him a quick nod, thanking him.

You still have to go in, he said.

I've never seen a Descendent up close. Should I be scared?

Tonium nodded.

Aidan stood at the base of the main mast, his shoulder resting against the tall wooden pole. The white, protuberant sails collected the warm breeze above the crew, moving the *Clíodhna* toward the emerging shore.

All twenty-eight men occupied the deck, listening to their captain. Their worried stares and fidgeting bodies made it clear they were not pirates, but a group of men pretending.

"This vessel," Aidan said, "is no longer a merchant ship employed by the Corwin Trading Company. We are not a hired crew, but men working for ourselves. With this, there is a new responsibility, and our seafaring positions must evolve with trust. If we steal or betray from this ship, then we take from ourselves."

"Aye!" men cheered.

"But like any system, we need order and those to uphold it. I nominate Mr. Nicholas Tillerson as quartermaster," Aidan said, pointing at his white-bearded friend.

Nicholas's downcast stare made it clear he thought he wasn't worthy of the job.

"If there is any other man whom this crew thinks is more suitable for the position, say his name," Aidan ordered.

The men turned to one another, waiting for the first to speak. But no other name arose from the group. Birds chirped in the distance.

"We shall vote. All in favor of Mr. Nicholas Tillerson as quartermaster, say aye!"

The crew erupted with "ayes" and raised hands.

Aidan nodded at his friend, who shook his head over the new title.

Thomas pushed his way to the front of the group. Stripped of his fancy clothes, he stood in the center of the crew, as one of them, in plain breeches and a white shirt.

"We never voted on a captain, Captain," Thomas declared.

Aidan's eyebrows knotted together. He should've thrown Thomas overboard.

"If this is a democratic crew, then we have to vote," Thomas added, staring at Aidan.

The sailor's shuffling feet and hushed whispers spread across the deck.

"Do you nominate yourself, Mr. Corwin?" Aidan asked, stepping toward him.

Thomas straightened. "Of course not. I nominate you."

Surprised, Aidan glanced over at Nicholas. The old man gaped, wide-eyed at Thomas's response.

Mr. Corwin spun, watching each man. "Captain Boyd has manned this ship with a kind and fair hand. He is young but born to lead. I nominate Mr. Aidan Boyd as captain."

Nicholas stepped into the circle of men. "I second that. The captain will remain our leader."

Thomas glanced over at Aidan, smirking. "Captain!"

Hands raised in the air. "Aye!" the crew cheered in unison.

Thomas stepped to Aidan's right side as the men continued to celebrate. "Always bury any doubt and make it clear who's in charge," Thomas whispered.

"I am in charge," Aidan said.

Thomas patted him on the back. "And I'll make sure they know that."

CHAPTER 26

Benlar swam deeper, following the others. Helo and Avia's home was made of elaborate tunnels branching out into a kitchen, bedroom, medical clinic, reading room, dining room — and that's only what they passed while swimming down into the earth.

Helo led the procession. Flashlights and gas lanterns lit their way to a door at the end of the passage. He retrieved a skeleton key with a decorative metal shell and unlocked the large door. Swinging it open, he swam through.

Avia followed, holding her leather medical bag with brass locks to her chest.

Benlar was last in the group. The light from his flashlight beamed into a dark space, never hitting the other side. He swam through the doorway into a giant cavern.

Helo unlocked a gold box mounted on the rock wall and lifted a switch, lighting the room.

Benlar glanced around. The room was massive and could hold a small city inside its belly.

Where are we? Piean asked, spinning to look at the hundreds of vessels parked on built-in platforms lining the sides of the chamber.

The heart of the mountain, Helo answered with no second thought, locking the door they came through.

How did you build this? Benlar asked.

He looked down. About sixty feet below, a train sat on a turntable. Its nose pointed toward an underground track.

Over time, Helo answered, swimming toward the long blue-and-black locomotive.

Piean poked Benlar's shoulder. *He has a train!*

I see it. Benlar pushed past her. *Where does it go?*

Avia swam next to Benlar, linking her arm with his. As a boy, Avia did this often with him and Mli, blaming her old age needed extra support. But now Avia's body was not old, but young and strong.

It will take us to Thessa, she said.

A direct route? Laza asked, swimming behind his mentor.

Yes, Helo answered, opening the steel door of the locomotive.

Benlar floated near the entrance, looking inside — his mouth agape.

Come, dear, Avia said, swimming through the door.

Benlar followed. The inside of the car put his home decor to shame. The painted ceiling gave life to a blue sky with a golden sunset. Four silver chandeliers hung every ten feet above the fully furnished living room car conjoined with the engineer's connected cabin. A cherry wood and mahogany compass was inlaid in the center of the wooden floor, then plastered with a clear sealant to protect it from the salt water. A polished silver star hung high on the north wall. More rooms filed behind a closed door.

Helo took the pilot's chair and turned on the train with the same skeleton key. Humming let the crew know the train was running.

Piean swam above Helo, examining the control panel. *It's not much different than our water vessel,* Piean said.

Simplicity is what makes a great machine. You might want to buckle up, Helo said, fastening his own belt, pinning himself to his chair.

Piean sat next to Laza on the other side of the room. Benlar took the seat next to Avia on a green baleen-haired sofa.

Avia leaned toward him. *How did she look? Was she all right?*

He nodded, locking the seatbelt over his lap. If this was a Thessian train, then it was built to be fast.

Did she remember you?

Not at first, Benlar answered.

I was there when Fiar gave her memory gas and stole her memories. I wanted to go with her, but I couldn't.

Why didn't you find me? I would've found her sooner. Benlar's voice cracked.

Avia grabbed his hand. *I didn't want her to be found.*

Why? he asked.

When she started to change, there was little time. I pushed her toward the shore on a wave. That old woman found her, and I watched as they took her into a house. She was safe there as long as Thessa believed she was still in the water.

You let her believe she belonged there.

It saved her. Avia grabbed the armrest as the train picked up speed.

Why didn't you go with her? Benlar asked.

I couldn't. I was hurt and unable to transform. Helo found me and put me into hibernation.

Piean leaned forward. *For how long?*

Avia's sweet face drifted into a frown after the interruption. *Four mouths.*

You're Mli's grandmother? You look no older than her, Piean said. *Except for your hair.*

That's the power of genetic rejuvenation. You can't tell how old anyone is by their appearance, Helo interjected into the conversation. *We'll be in Thessa in two hours.* Unbuckling, Helo swam to the living room car and pointed at Benlar and Piean. *You two come with me.*

Why? Benlar asked.

Because you don't have much time to familiarize yourself with my weapons and water vessel. Once we're in Thessa, everyone needs to be ready to fight.

Jocelyn's arms draped around Tonium's neck as he carried her out of the water vessel and into Thessa's cathedral. Jocelyn peered up, and the world seemed smaller under the massive structure. Gas lamps lit the ocean floor in a constant glow, blending day and night.

Three other soldiers surrounded her and Tonium as they swam through the open doors. Hundreds of merpeople moved around the first floor, each busy with an important task to help run Thessa.

Mental conversations were kept quiet, leaving an unnatural silence. No one looked at her twice. She wondered how many had been brought into the cathedral, drugged and paralyzed.

Jocelyn glanced around the room, counting the exits. One near the south end, guarded by three mermen. Another in the north end was closed off by glass doors. The largest exit stood the way they'd come. The main entrance to the building flowed with merrows, making it hard to secure, but it was also the most visible.

She held her breath. How was she going to get out of here?

One of the soldiers slid open a gate to a steam-pulled elevator. Tonium swam in first with her in his arms. Her fin scraped on the seaweed-molded metal gate.

Sorry, Tonium said.

I couldn't feel it, Jocelyn lied.

Should we give her another dose? She's able to use her hands, an observant guard asked.

Tonium squeezed her tighter, lifting her another inch. *No. We don't want to intubate again. Inam wants to talk with her, not dissect her.*

But they want her sedated. Fiar was adamant, the quiet guard added, twisting a knob for the forty-second floor.

The elevator moved, shifting the water downward. One of the mermen smelled of honey. The tails of the guards hit the floor as the elevator moved up.

Switched on hyperdrive, Jocelyn's heart thudded in her chest. Fiar! The merman who'd dragged her father into the center of Thessa to execute him in front of a crowd, who'd slit her mother's throat in front of her, who'd taken her memories —Fiar could be waiting for her, ready to strike. She gripped Tonium's leather collar of his vest. Every fiber of her was ready to fight.

The elevator slowed.

If she wanted to kill Fiar, she needed to control the ocean, but its voice was absent.

A guard slid open the gate, grinding on its track. One by one the guards swam out, clearing the way for Tonium and Jocelyn.

The room could fit ten of Aidan's ships side by side and

had an opal balcony overlooking the city. Thousands of merrows could fit in this room with enough space to fit another thousand. Eight gold chairs, arranged in a crescent shape, faced Jocelyn. Five of them were occupied.

Jocelyn squinted to see faces, but she could only make out tail colors. Two yellows sat together, with a gold in the middle, a red tail on its right, and a light blue by its side.

The troop swam across the empty room toward the faceless Descendants.

Where are you? Jocelyn called out to the ocean, but it remained silent amid the shadows of the hundred or so glass lanterns lighting the room.

Stop! a merman's voice boomed over everyone's mind.

The soldiers stopped in the middle of the room. Jocelyn squeezed tighter to Tonium. He seemed to be her only hope.

Is the girl sedated? the voice asked.

The mean guard swam forward, adjusting his armor.

She's conscious, but the blue ring venom is in effect, he stated in a business-like tone. *We can give her another dose if you like.*

Every muscle in Jocelyn's body tightened, ready to flee out of the open balcony. Tonium held tighter to her. He was a good merman, but he worked for Thessa. Jocelyn knew he would finish his job.

No, I wish to speak to her, and if she's drugged into a coma, we'll miss a rare opportunity. Bring her, the merman ordered.

The guards moved forward, and the Descendants came into focus.

The merwoman and merman with yellow tails held hands. Their golden chairs were trimmed with pearls along the top like crowns. They appeared in their forties, but Jocelyn figured they were much older.

A young merman, no more than twenty, sat in the center.

His hands gripped the armrests as he sat on the edge of his seat, his gold tail flicking the water. A merwoman in her sixties sat to his right. She flattened her red dress against her red tail.

The merman with the light-blue fin rested his head against the back of his chair, bored. He seemed to be in his forties too, but Jocelyn couldn't be sure. The youngest was in charge. He had to be Inam.

The young merman swam away from his chair and drifted toward Jocelyn, his face in awe.

You've aged, Inam said, reaching his hand toward her, but he pulled back before he touched her skin.

Inam waved, and two mermaids swam from a dark corner, carrying a gold-leafed chair. They placed it beside Tonium, then swam off, hiding in the shadows.

Inam motioned toward the chair. Tonium gently set Jocelyn in it and returned to his regiment, a solder again.

Jocelyn slumped in the seat, forcing her body to appear paralyzed, but she couldn't stop her lip from quivering. She studied her host's face. His black hair layered down to his chin, matching his eyes.

They call you Mli, correct? he asked.

The other Descendants leaned forward, listening to Inam question her.

She nodded.

The young merman's face lit up with a wide smile. *I assume you know I'm Inam.*

She nodded again, holding her voice, afraid it would give her away that she was scared of them.

Inam swam around her. He picked up her black hair and rubbed it between his fingers. *This is new.*

Jocelyn glanced up at him. His face was inches from hers. *Do you know me?* she asked.

The smile on Inam's face slipped into one of disbelief. Even the bored Descendant peered down at her.

I have waited an eternity to hear your voice, Inam said, swimming to face her and taking her hands.

Eternity? Jocelyn's voice shook. *What do you mean eternity?*

The young merman petted her hands. *My dear child, you are perfect. Flawless.*

The other Descendants nodded in agreement. Jocelyn peered at them. A flicker of yellow light caught her eye, and she noticed another gold chair behind the eight, concealed in the corner.

How do you know me, and why am I here? Jocelyn asked, anger flooding her voice.

We brought you here to protect you. To take care of you, the red-tailed merwoman stated, her voice a loud chirp.

How can you protect me? Your merman killed my family.

They weren't your family, Inam said.

Jocelyn glared at him. *Of course they were. Fiar killed my mother and father...*

No. He killed the ones who'd kidnapped you. We brought you back, safe. And here you are. Inam ran his finger down her bruised nose, barely touching her skin.

Jocelyn moved away from his touch.

I see the venom has worn off a lot faster than predicted. Are you going to be a good girl, or are we going to need to give you more? Inam asked, pulling away.

Anger churning in her stomach, Jocelyn lifted from the chair, towering over him. *You lie. They were my parents!*

Inam swam back, distancing himself from her. *No. They weren't,* he said, before giving a nod.

Jocelyn spun around. Tonium was there. He embraced her seconds before jabbing a needle into her forearm.

Everything went dark as she sank into his arms.

A swarm of kelp gulls circled among the three masts, squawking at each other. A few brave ones landed on deck, begging for food, but were shooed away with haste.

Banana and palm trees covered the rim of an overgrown forest. The light-blue waters surrounding Madagascar washed over its white beaches, almost touching wooden huts scattered along the shore. Larger structures topped the tree line. Jolly boats rested in the sand, ready to take sailors back to their anchored ships moored in the shallow port.

Aidan ordered his men to lay anchor and selected a handful of them to accompany him to shore. Nicholas was left to manage the ship with strict orders to set sail if any danger arose.

It had been six years since Aidan's first and only visit to Libertalia. New to the Corwin Trading Company, he was well informed of life at sea, and Baron Christopher Corwin had taken a liking to him. Soon the fourteen-year-old was shadowing the master of the ship, learning to read, write, and captain a crew. Master Corwin's kindness reminded Aidan of the father he missed. The years of mentoring aged Aidan quickly, when in fact, he was still a young man.

Aidan descended the dangling Jacob's ladder from the deck into the swaying rowboat, joining his small crew — Thomas among them. The small vessel rubbed against its larger counterpart.

"You are to stay onboard," Aidan's rough voice ordered Thomas.

The men stared at their former employer.

"You need someone who knows business," Thomas said, looking rather plain without a cravat around his neck.

"I am capable of doing business, Mr. Corwin." Aidan tilted up his leather tricorne hat.

"Yes, you are quite capable, *but* you did not attend Eton and Balliol College, studying business to ready yourself for the family trade. I did. And you want the smartest person in the room on your side." Thomas kicked an oar toward a man. "Shall we?"

Aidan exhaled. Thomas had a point.

"Onward," he said, pushing off from the merchant ship before sitting at the bow of the small watercraft.

His men released the ropes that secured the rowboat to the ship, sank their oars into the water, and rowed toward Libertalia.

CHAPTER 27

The car wobbled on its tracks as the train sped through the underground tunnel toward Thessa. Helo led Piean and Benlar through the sleeping quarters, housed with four bunk beds, to a back door.

The merman pushed it open and switched on a light. Crammed in the space was a new water vessel, its polished brass surface uncorroded by the salt of the sea.

That's a Sailfish! Piean clapped her hands.

Can you drive it? Helo asked, swimming to the top of the submarine and unlatching the hatch.

Yes. Her voice peaked with excitement.

Good. We'll need a driver. Do you know Thessa? Helo secured the door to stay open.

Piean shook her head. *I've never been there.*

Then you are of no use, the merman said.

The mermaid's hands dropped to her side.

Helo pointed to Benlar. *Do you know the city?*

Benlar nodded. *I attended school there.*

Good. You're a landwalker?

Yes.

Come. Helo dove into the vessel.

Benlar followed the merman, swimming past Piean. The girl's shoulders slumped forward. He turned to face her. She stared at the ground. Benlar could see the hurt in her downcast eyes.

Can you really drive this? he asked.

Glancing up, Piean pointed to the hood of the vessel. *It's a faster version of Laza's. The piloting systems are pretty much the same.*

How do you know that? he asked.

I don't just read fiction.

Benlar grabbed her hand. *Come on.*

She slipped her hand from his. *Helo's right. My not knowing the city could get us all killed.*

Thessa runs in spirals. Everything leads to the Cathedral. And if you get lost, or trapped, you drive up.

But everyone will see us, she said.

You can outrun them. I'm good at driving, but for some reason, I believe you're better.

A blush tinged Piean's cheeks. *Really?*

Yeah. Benlar's heart skipped while he looked at her. He wanted to take her hand just to hold it, but he stopped himself. He turned away from her, swimming toward the open hatch. *And I wasn't trained to sit and wait. I'm going after Mli.*

Piean swam behind him. *So you really believe I'm better than you?*

The *Clíodhna* shifted with the ocean in the distance. Seagulls squawked, fighting each other for remnants of some dead creature on the sandy beach.

When Aidan jumped into the shallow tide, the water

splashed over the top of his boots. He trudged out of the sea, leaving three of his crew to pull the jolly boat onto shore.

A horn blew for the third time from a watchtower overlooking the port. A group of men emerged from an opening in the trees—their swords drawn and pistols aimed.

"I'm in search of your king," Aidan said, raising his hands into the air. His crew followed his lead.

The man in the front of the pack shook his head, swaying dreadlocks framing his face. "Ye turn around and go back from where ye came." His pistol pointed at Aidan's face.

Aidan stared at the company of pirates. Most of their hair was uncombed and wild, their flesh weathered by the sun's heat. Three of the five men were dark skinned.

"The yellow fish swims toward the northern horizon." Aidan lowered his raised hand and touched his forehead.

An older, red-bearded man in the back of the group, his waist vest a vibrant green, lowered his sword. "Wot did he say?" he asked in a thick French accent.

Aidan raised his voice. "The yellow fish swims toward the northern horizon."

The man pushed to the front of the group as his men kept their aim.

"As dee blue fish swims toward dee Southern 'orizon," the man said, touching his forehead in the same secret gesture. "Are you Christopher's son?"

Aidan shook his head. "He was my mentor."

"He was my father," Thomas spoke up.

The man stared at Thomas. "You look like him. Put your weapons down," he ordered his men.

They lowered their weapons but remained ready to strike.

"I am Captain Augustus LaValle, King of Libertalia. We shall talk. Come this way." The man walked toward the jungle.

Aidan and his crew followed Captain LaValle as the other pirates circled around them, making it clear they were not welcomed guests.

Muffled voices came and went in a dense fog of dream and reality. Jocelyn rolled her head as a metallic aftertaste invaded her dry tongue. A radiant light seeped through the thin surface of her closed eyelids in a red tint and warmed her skin. There was a burnt smell to the water.

Jocelyn squinted her eyes, allowing them to adjust to the overly lit room. She lifted her arm, but it wouldn't move from the cold porcelain tray she lay on. Kelp straps held her arms and tail in place.

Inam sat beside the medical table, petting her hair. His smile was caring, almost loving.

Two mermaid healers swam around the hibernation room, Thessa's symbol printed on their matching gray baleen vests. Jocelyn counted eight hibernation chambers behind Inam. The glass lid covers gave clear view to three faces sedated, in a coma, as their bodies turned back time.

Shaking her head, the residuals of the drug blurred her vision. *I know what I am.*

Do you now? Inam asked, amusement in his voice.

Jocelyn stared at him. For someone older than civilization, he was rather attractive. His boyish eyes were innocent, but she knew it was a lie. Deep down, she knew him.

You don't know what I can do. Let me go, and I won't hurt you, Jocelyn said, trying to pull her hand from the cuffs.

I can't do that.

You don't understand. I can control —

The ocean, Inam interrupted her.

Jocelyn's eyes widened, and she stopped struggling with the straps.

I've watched you grow from an infant to an adult over and over, only missing your voice. I understand why he did what he did, Inam said, taking her hand.

Who? Jocelyn asked.

I know him as Philo, but you know him as Helo.

My grandfather?

It's funny he took that role while raising you, when in fact, he is a child compared to you.

Clarity cleared her vision as curiosity took over, blocking the effects of the drug. *What do you mean?* she asked.

Inam glanced at the healers. *Leave us.*

His workers bowed before swimming out of the room, shutting the door behind them. Jocelyn and Inam were alone, with only sleeping ears listening.

Years ago, too many to count, my grandfather met your pregnant mother when he was a young merman.

Jocelyn's heart stopped for a moment, blocking her from speaking.

Your mother was not from our land or world but another, far away, yet remarkably close. She traveled with the help of a small creature who gave her the gift of flight. The creature left her with a promise to return but never did. When my grandfather found her, your mother was being sold as a mage, her gift for manipulating water raising her value.

Jocelyn stared up at the tube of light on the ceiling. *The mage and the fish.*

Yes, but the legend is different from the truth. She didn't make a dress of scales or drink mermaid tears. She was never the first mermaid. You were. When my father bought her, she was pregnant with you.

That can't be.

Her stomach turned, knowing she was lying to herself. Her life was a mirage to keep her at bay. A way to control her.

A man of science, my grandfather and eight of his colleagues studied her as she gained more power throughout pregnancy. A child from her land, she had a father whom your mother said could change his appearance into anything he wished. One night, she escaped and ran to the beach and into the sea. They found her dead three days later, but you were still alive.

Inam's eyes moved across Jocelyn's face.

They removed you from her. Born with a tail and gills, you transformed in front of them. You grew legs, and your lungs developed to breathe out of the water with a simple whimper.

The pieces of Laza's research fell into place. Jocelyn closed her eyes. The old merman knew she was the key to Thessa's beginnings.

That is why you can change. My blood is in the medallions.

Inam clapped his hands. *Beautiful and smart. My grandfather injected himself with your blood. The transformation was painful, but it worked. Metamorphosis only lasted the duration of the battling cells. His versus yours. Human against whatever you are. Ours always won. They created the medallion to house your DNA.*

Jocelyn's pulse pounded in the water.

The ocean was a plaything for my grandfather and his colleagues. They went to the sea, learning from the creatures under the water. My father was first to discover the Turritopsis Dohrnii, but the jellyfish's ability to de-age wasn't applied to our kind until my brother and I took over after his passing. We spent our true years perfecting hibernation, but it didn't work without your DNA. This world doesn't work without you.

Jocelyn shook her head. *How old am I?*

More than four thousand years.

Sickness bubbled in her stomach. *You locked me away, draining me.*

No. The pain in Inam's voice brought Jocelyn to look at him. *You did it yourself. You chose to hibernate after you sank Atlantis. You sank our home. Killed our families.*

Panic rushed over her, sending chills.

Inam inhaled. Pain fogged his dark eyes. *Only nine survived from your destruction,* he said, blinking away his memories.

No.

Yes. Inam grabbed her hand. *You were like a grandmother to us. What Philo did was cruel to bring you back.*

My grandfather?

Inam nodded. *My bother. Your watcher and a Descendant—one of the eight survivors of Atlantis.*

My life.

A lie.

I haven't hurt anyone.

You will. You will never be strong enough to control your powers. As you get older, they will consume you. Then you'll crush this world with a wave of your hand, just as you did to Atlantis.

Panic turned into anger, heating her blood. Jocelyn locked eyes with Inam. *I'm assuming you'd like me to go back into hibernation.*

Inam squeezed her hand. *Yes.*

Jocelyn moved her head closer to him. *I don't believe you. I'm not a monster,* she whispered.

Grinning, Inam swam over to a table lined with syringes and pick one up with yellow liquid inside. *When I was a child, you would sing a lullaby to us, with words unknown to any merman.*

With a flat, deep voice, he began to hum.

The melody swirled in her mind as the ocean replaced Inam's low tones with its harmonic voice—singing to her.

Small electrical pulses zapped Jocelyn's skin as the water swayed over her. It was here with her. Listening. Waiting. The ocean sat idle, wanting her permission to possess her. To give her endless power with a brief moment of self-sacrifice. She had the power to call it to the surface, but pain and hatred were what fueled it.

Lifting her chin, Jocelyn closed her eyes and breathed in the ocean, becoming one with it. Energy sparked within her. Before she demanded freedom, Inam slid the syringe into her neck, and the world went black.

But the ocean moved through her, reminding her she was alive.

CHAPTER 28

A dirt road weaved through the trees and into a city of structures raised by low stilts. Feral dogs ran along the buildings, searching for food and companions. At the end of the street, drunken men stumbled, either alone or with vibrantly dressed women on their arms, from a grand building with a thatched roof.

Captain LaValle swaggered up the steps of the brothel and into the establishment. Eyes turned from bought romance, and swollen lips pulled away from one another to acknowledge their king's arrival. The room quieted with each click of his heeled boot.

Pirates parted for Captain Augustus LaValle and his group as they made their way to the back courtyard—open to the forest cascading over the buildings and into the pirate colony. The few occupying the space left without orders.

LaValle sat at a small round table. His men grabbed wooded chairs from empty tables and positioned them in front of their leader.

Aidan sat first, removing his hat and placing it on the table. His crew stood behind him, unwilling to lose their footing in case of a fight.

Clay bricks and red dirt covered the floor of the quadrangle. Above, two balconies faced each other. A well-dressed woman peered down from one. A long cigarette was clenched between her teeth as the smoke encircled her head. She bowed her head to LaValle, then shut the wooden door tight. Aidan suspected she was the Madame, if there was one.

"I am sorry to 'ear about Baron Corwin." LaValle put a fist over his heart. "He was a true *ami*." He glanced at Thomas. "You now dee baron?"

"Yes," Thomas answered.

"*Oui*," Lavalle mocked, laughter following. "Tell me, what brings you to my Libertalia?"

Thomas took the seat next to Aidan.

"We seek your help," Aidan answered.

"Oh, I see," the pirate king said, leaning back in his chair. The sea-green ruffles of his sleeve collapsed against his arm as he stroked his stringy beard.

A painted woman entered the courtyard with a platter resting on her head. With a graceful bow, she slid the tray onto the table. The sweet and sour aroma of pineapple and papaya permeated the space. Placing a pewter mug in front of LaValle, the lady filled his cup from a pitcher. Aidan smelled the scent of banana rum.

The woman retreated, leaving LaValle to decide who he deemed worthy to drink with him.

Thomas shifted forward. "My father was a businessman, as I assume you are…"

Captain Lavalle's cold stare found Thomas. "Your father was more dan a businessman."

Sweat rose at Aidan's hairline. Thomas's impatience would get them killed.

"Of course. He was a great man who helped you…"

"Can you believe dis man?" Lavalle asked, pointing his jagged fingernail at Thomas.

The king's men grunted and grinned.

The situation had soured for the worse. Aidan had to gain control.

"You speak as if you knew your father, but you know nothing. But *I* know what you are and what you are not. And you are no son of Master Corwin, and no equal to mine."

Thomas shook his head, licking his bottom lip.

"How are your wife and daughter?" Aidan spoke up.

The pirate king took a drink, studying Aidan. "I remember you. An *enfant* dee time you came. A boy in training and now a man. What do I call you?" LaValle tapped the end of the fork on the table.

"Captain Boyd," Aidan answered, his voice wavering.

LaValle smiled as he ate a pineapple. "I remember dee boy as Mr. Boyd. Not captain, but we all must become men at some point." LaValle waved a finger, and a shorter man rushed forward. The pirate poured Aidan a drink and retreated. "Dey are doing well," LaValle said.

"We were friends, your daughter and I."

"I remember."

"They would not be here without Baron Corwin's assistance in escorting them from France."

"You also played a role, claiming dem as your mother and sister. Lying to the authorities. You were young but brave. My Adalene still speaks of your kindness."

"I ask you to return the favor," Aidan said.

LaValle squinted, wrinkling his brow. "What trouble are you in?"

"He took my ship," Thomas hissed.

The courtyard roared with laughter.

"You stole a ship from your employer, and you keep him on board?" LaValle chuckled.

Anger boiled in Aidan. He would not be a joke to these men. He slammed his fist on the table, quieting the rowdy laughter. "The British Navy killed my friend, and I lost the only woman I have ever loved to the sea. Do not dare laugh at me."

LaValle scratched his chin, silent, before nodding. "What do you need?"

The tight underground tunnel opened to another large cavern. The train crawled to a stop on a turntable. Sand settled around the metal wheels as steam fogged the water.

In the floor of the sleeping compartment, Helo lifted the wooden boards to uncover an arsenal of weaponry. Benlar picked up a Thessian-issued crossbow, its range far better than his, and strapped it to his utility belt. Stocking arrows and methane clathrate, Benlar and the others filled every ring and pouch with military-grade weapons. Helo was much more than a lecturer, but Benlar would wait to question him until Mli was safe.

The five crowded into the Sailfish watercraft. Piean manned the helm with maps of the city spread around her. During the two-hour ride, Piean had studied, memorizing the two-dimensional city.

Helo cranked a lever on the control panel, opening the back of the train car.

Reversing, Piean steered the vessel into the opening. She tilted the wheel back and drifted over the train. In the center of the cave, the locomotive rested on a cross of tracks, which led to four tunnels.

Where do they go? Benlar asked.

Everywhere, Helo answered, pointing up. *There.*

Piean directed the craft up the walls of the cavern to an opening. She glanced over at Helo, then Benlar. Her rigid grip on the wheel whitened her knuckles, making it clear she was scared.

Thessa is above us, and we only have one chance to claim Mli. There is no place for fear. Count to three. Breathe. Then go, Helo ordered, patting her shoulder.

Where in Thessa are we? Benlar asked, examining the rocky cliff of the cavern and the dark hole in front of them.

Under the Cathedral, Helo stated. Avia took his hand. Helo kissed hers.

Who are you? Benlar asked.

Laza called from the back. *He's a Descendant.*

Benlar's mouth dropped.

No way, Piean stated.

That's why you stayed old and never hibernated when I was a child. You look like him, Benlar said.

Who? Piean asked.

Inam, Benlar said.

My brother.

You knew! he yelled at Avia.

Mli's grandmother swam in front of Helo. *Benlar, you don't understand.*

No, I don't. Inform me.

Piean rose from her chair, pointing over his shoulder at Avia and Helo. *And you better do it quickly,* Piean added.

Laza shook his head. *Sit down.*

No, I agree with Benlar. We need answers now.

Helo guided his wife out of harm's way, standing tall in front of Piean and Benlar. His black tail kicked against the metal grate of the vessel's flooring.

She woke, and I couldn't put her to sleep again. We raised her as family, hiding her from Thessa and the Descendants. But without her, our race cannot survive. Thessa would fall, and we will go extinct without her blood. Inam would never allow that to happen. I knew it was only time until he sent his army, but I was hoping for more.

Laza drifted up. *I was right. She is the child.*

She is the mother of us all, Helo said.

What do you plan to do with her? Benlar asked.

I wanted her to have a choice and not be trapped in a box, never allowed to die.

Benlar studied Helo. The merman loved Mli. Benlar nodded at Piean. *Take us to Thessa.*

The girl dropped to her chair, yanking the steering wheel back. She sped the water vessel into the opening.

The darkness weaved into her mind. The ocean's song became her sanity. Wiping away the distortion of man and merrow, leaving a clear vision of light in the grayness. She was no longer Mli or Jocelyn, but more. The tips of her fingers pushed against the current, but as soon as she gained a little control, they injected her again. She sank deeper into the abyss, once again drowning. Not from the water that embraced her, but from Thessa's cold touch.

The power within burned her heart, searing its edges in ash and pain. If she woke, two would live within this body. She and the ocean.

CHAPTER 29

Clouds clustered above swaying trees. The crisp scent of wet land turned Aidan's head. Gray lines streaked the darkening sky as rain fell over the south of Madagascar. Blue skies blanketed above Libertalia with small, scattered black clouds blowing north. The heavy rain was coming, but for now, the sun kissed the dry dirt.

Captain Augustus LaValle led Aidan and Thomas through the small city. A random droplet hit the top of Aidan's hat. At the outskirts, they came upon a modest two-story home settled under the canopy of the forest. Tilled soil lined the side yard in rows of seeded dirt.

"Welcome to *ma maison*," LaValle said, climbing the steps to his home.

A buzzing mosquito flew by Aidan's ear. He swatted it away before the insect could land.

Thomas's dismay slumped his shoulders. Aidan knew Thomas wished to stay with the other men to taste the goods of Libertalia, but LaValle had given a nonnegotiable invitation to dine at his home.

The rusting iron hinges ground as LaValle opened his door and walked in. Removing his hat, Aidan followed.

Floral wallpaper with gold and pink butterflies covered the entry walls. Large paintings of stone castles and quaint cottages, shielded by the remarkable beauty of vibrant trees, hung on every wall. A reminder of LaValle's homeland— France.

LaValle marched through the house to the reading room. Mint silk drapes decorated the long windows. The baroque furniture matched the curtains, with mint leaves painted on the fabric. Two women sat on a settee.

"My loves, *nous avons de la visite*," LaValle spoke in French. We have visitors.

The older of the two lifted her eyes from her embroidery. Her powered white hair paled her aging skin. "*Mari*," she said, lifting her hand for her husband.

LaValle paraded over the Persian rug and took her hand. He kissed it before helping her to her feet. "Gentlemen, my *très belle* wife, Lady Élise, and my daughter, Adalene."

LaValle waved his hand toward the young woman still sitting on the sofa, studying Aidan. Pink bows decorated her blonde curls pulled to the top of her head. Above her lips, a drawn-in beauty spot marked her pale skin. The embroidery rested on her lap, and she held the threaded needle suspended between her fingers.

"Mr. Boyd and Mr. Corwin." Lavalle introduced them to his family.

"I know you," Adalene said, her eyes locked on Aidan.

Aidan bowed his head. "Hello, Adalene."

Adalene dropped the embroidery onto a side table, leaped to her feet, and ran to Aidan, wrapping her arms around his neck. Her blonde curls pressed against his cheek.

"My Aidan! You have come back." Her French accent was prominent as she wept.

The pirate king glared at the man embraced by his only daughter. Aidan made sure to keep his arms locked at his side.

Adalene stared up at him. She ran a finger down the side of his face. "You are a boy no more. You have aged."

"So have you," Aidan answered.

"Dee boy is a captain now," Lavalle stated, linking his arms with his wife's.

"*Non*, you will still be my Aidan."

Adalene kissed his cheek before releasing him. She faced Thomas. Her red lips lifted in a smile.

"My lady," Thomas said, taking the young woman's hand and kissing it.

"You must be a Corwin," Adalene said, her eyes widening from the attention of a well-bred English man.

"I am." Thomas slipped his hand from hers.

"What brings you to our island?" Adalene asked.

"Dey wish to become pirates," Lavalle stated with a boyish grin.

Adalene turned toward Aidan. "A pirate. How adventurous. Are you to teach dem, Papa?"

Lavalle nodded, escorting his wife back to the sofa. The two sat together.

"We just need time to ready our ship and purchase weaponry," Aidan clarified.

Adalene grabbed Aidan's hand and led him to another sofa. She sat, pulling him beside her. "I cannot believe you are back. I thought I would never see you again, but here you are."

"Here I am," Aidan repeated, shifting away from the nearness of her leg. The freckled child he had befriended fourteen years ago had grown into a beautiful young woman.

Thomas occupied an armchair.

"We would also like to careen our ship while here." Aidan

directed the conversation back to LaValle.

"Dere is a careenage to dee south. We will go at high tide tomorrow, and your men can work," the pirate king said.

"*Merci,*" Aidan said, playing with the brim of his tricorne hat, the leather worn smooth.

Adalene grabbed the hat and placed it on a side table. She slid her hands into his.

Surprised, Aidan froze.

"You made a promise to me. Do you remember?" Her green eyes searched his.

Aidan shook his head. The last time he'd seen Adalene, she was a twelve-year-old girl desperate to fall in love. Something she seemed not to have grown out of.

"What type of promise?" Thomas asked, leaning forward.

Adalene's smile brightened the room. "Dee stars," the girl cooed.

The memory of the young girl weeping in the corner of a ship, holding tight to a porcelain doll with matching blonde ringlets fluttered into his mind. Adalene had boarded Baron Corwin's ship with little knowledge of the situation at hand. Her father, a sought-after pirate, unable to come himself, only sent a letter with his crest melted in wax. Worried his family would be used as bait to lure him from hiding, LaValle requested they leave for Madagascar with a man they'd never met. Abandoning their former lives, Adalene and her mother hid in the belly of the ship until France disappeared in mist.

As the stars lit the sky, night after night, Aidan promised to take one from her homeland back to her when he returned. A gift he knew he could never give.

"How romantic," Thomas said.

"We were young," Aidan quickly added, embarrassed Thomas now knew one of his personal memories. "I wish to depart in less than three days."

"Dat can be arranged. Do you have any form of payment?" LaValle asked, bringing the conversation back to business.

"Yes," Aidan said, slipping his hands from Adalene's and focusing on her father.

From the corner of his eyes, Aidan could see Thomas staring at the pirate king's daughter.

"What form?" LaValle asked.

"Silks and spices from India," Aidan spoke, leaning to block Thomas's view.

LaValle patted his knee. "Good boy. Den we can trade. What kind of weapons?"

"Cannons. Swords and pistols, one for each of my crewmembers."

LaValle stared at Aidan. "Enough to hook a ship?"

Aidan looked to the ground and nodded.

A lamp above the nose of the Sailfish watercraft lit the way through the steep tunnel. Jutting rocks reached for the submarine but never touched its metal shell. Piean gripped the wheel as she leaned close to the windshield.

Movement from what looked like seaweed shadowed the end of the tunnel.

Benlar inhaled, checking the trigger of the crossbow once again. It clicked back with little effort. He was ready to fight.

What do I do? Piean asked.

Drive through it, Helo directed.

Benlar left Piean's side and swam toward the group in the back.

Avia's long, gray hair parted over her shoulders. She reached out and took Benlar's hands. The young merwoman before him was still the old merwoman who looked after Mli and him while they played, watching them grow.

She's still my light, Avia said.

I know, Benlar answered.

Helo turned to Laza, who cradled his weapon in his arms. *You stay with Piean.*

Laza nodded with quick agreement.

The watercraft's nose separated the stringy seaweed.

What is this place? Piean asked.

Rusted trains lay abandoned on a useless track. Leaking motor oil played with their light.

The old train system. Go right, Helo ordered.

Piean's eyes widened. *I didn't know there was one.*

You wouldn't. Remember where the tunnel is, child. Helo spoke to Piean.

She nodded to the passengers in the back.

Helo unbraided his hair then rebraided it, a nervous habit. *They'll keep her in the medical wing of the Cathedral.*

Piean pressed the gas, kicked the submarine to the right, and followed the abandoned track.

Are we going to just swim in? Benlar asked.

Helo glanced at him. *Hell, no. The Cathedral is heavily guarded at all times. No one can enter or leave without their knowing. If we swim half a mile's radius from the structure, we'll be dead.*

Being uninformed raised the hair on Benlar's arms. *Then what is your plan?*

We go inside it.

What? Benlar asked.

When I built this structure, I made sure there was a way out. There's enough room between the walls for one to travel unnoticed.

Piean glanced back. *You're that old?*

Ignoring the girl, Helo pointed. *There will be a mine shaft to the left. Take it, but go slow.*

All right, Piean said. She leaned closer to the windshield, searching for the turn.

When we find her, there's a chance she will not be Mli anymore.

Avia's worried eyes darted to her husband. *Will you be able to bring her back?*

I don't know, Helo answered.

What do you mean? How can she not be Mli? Benlar's voice heated with anger.

Avia continued to hold Benlar's hand.

If she is hurt or threatened, there's a possibility she'll surrender to her powers. And if that happens, she could disappear, Helo said.

And if she does? Benlar asked.

The vehicle slowed and turned into the mine shaft.

Helo unbraided his hair again. *We face the ocean, and she is a cruel spirit.*

Jocelyn's naked human body was exposed to the sun but numb to the elements. She stared into the black eyes of the mermaid floating in front of her. Jocelyn's toes grazed the cold moss as she drifted above the ground.

"I see you," the mermaid sang.

"And I you," Jocelyn replied.

The mermaid smiled and reached for Jocelyn, but she refused to give the merrow what she wanted.

"I can protect us," the mermaid pleaded.

Jocelyn shook her head. "I'm afraid of what you'll do."

The merrow's expression darkened as she grabbed Jocelyn's face, burning Jocelyn's skin with her touch. "We are one, you and I. But you still fight. Why?"

"Because I'm stronger than you," Jocelyn answered.

The mermaid pulled back, whipping her auburn hair against Jocelyn's cheek. "No, you're not."

Something bit Jocelyn's neck, and blackness melted everything away.

CHAPTER 30

The headlamp on the Sailfish shut off, leaving everything in darkness. Benlar flicked on his flashlight. His beam was soon accompanied by four more.

Laza's shook. Piean smirked at him. She knew he was never brave outside of his comfort zones.

Helo unlatched the hatch above the pilot's seat. *Keep to the dark.*

Laza flicked off his flashlight.

I don't think anyone will come down here. This mine has been abandoned for centuries, but don't take the risk. Piean —Helo looked at the mermaid still sitting in the driver's seat— *keep the engine warm but quiet. If we're followed, you'll need to be ready.*

Piean nodded.

Ready? Helo asked Avia and Benlar.

Yeah, Benlar answered, swallowing his fear, forcing it down with his anger.

Helo swam out of the vessel with Avia at his tail.

Benlar followed, but Piean grabbed his arm as he swam by. She found his eyes, and for a brief moment, Benlar thought she would weep. But instead, she pulled him to her and kissed his lips.

He began to protest and pull away, but he couldn't. He leaned into her touch.

Pulling away, Piean kissed his forehead. *Just in case you don't come back,* she whispered.

Benlar couldn't help but laugh. *That's reassuring.*

Piean took his hand. *Goodbye, Benlar.*

He smiled at her before swimming through the door.

Piean sank into her seat. Even if he returned safely, he would still be fighting for Mli, and she would remain the girl from Ommo. The unwanted. Piean ran her finger around the steering wheel. But then again, he had returned her kiss...

The hatch closed above her. Piean swam up and locked the Sailfish.

The stale water tasted like copper.

Benlar's light illuminated Helo and Avia digging away at a pile of rusted metal at the base of an algae-covered rock wall. Avia pushed a coral-encrusted train wheel away from her. It rolled into the red sand before falling to its side, dispersing a cloud of dust. A longneck eel slithered from the debris in search of another hiding spot.

Digging in, Benlar kept one hand on his flashlight. He lifted the heavy material away until an opening in the wall was revealed. The three of them heaved the last of the forgotten metal that once ran along Thessa's travel system hundreds of years before, clearing the entry.

Helo went first. His black fin swept up the dormant silt. Avia swam through the fogged water, the beam of her flashlight glittering off the floating sand.

Thessa was a fortress filled with trained killers willing to give up their lives to keep the Descendants safe. The click of an arrow sliding into the barrel and the string tightening reassured Benlar he had some type of control. He swam into the dark tunnel with two knives, twenty-four arrows, a crossbow, and a flashlight. Swallowing back the aftertaste of adrenalin pumping through him, he counted his breaths, quieting his heart. He focused on Avia's gray hair swaying with the water as they ascended.

The width of the tunnel closed inward. The tips of the bow scratched against the white stone—catching. There was no mistaking they were somewhere in the Cathedral. Reluctant, Benlar removed the arrow, folded his crossbow, and locked it to a ring on his belt. Their once-quick pace slowed to a crawl as the space around them hugged their bodies, prohibiting them from using their tails to swim forward.

Digging his fingertips into the ridged white limestone, Benlar propelled himself up, climbing the walls—his flashlight clanging against the hard surface.

For what seemed like hours, the three moved. The sharp, unkempt surface of the rock tore at their skin.

I need to stop, Avia whispered, her voice hoarse from the physical strain.

Benlar pressed his back and tail against the wall to keep from sinking. His muscles tingled as they relaxed. *How much farther?* Benlar asked, unable to see anything more than the bottom of Avia's fin.

We're almost there, Helo's clear voice answered. *We need to keep going.*

Avia's tail patted the water, but she didn't move. *What if she's not there? What if they took her somewhere else?* The worry in Avia's voice matched what was in Benlar's heart.

They wouldn't do that.

How do you know? Benlar replied to Helo.

The best of everything is here. They wouldn't risk putting her anywhere else, Helo said.

The pain of the rock digging into Benlar's hip had him shift down, piercing new skin. *How did you get her out the first time?* Benlar asked.

I didn't. Over time, Thessa's citizens got restless, and an uprising tried to gain power. They targeted the Cathedral. We couldn't risk her being discovered. Helo's deep voice filled Benlar's mind. *We voted on moving her. We had enough blood stored away to last decades.* He shifted up.

Pebbles flaked from the wall as Avia moved with him, landing in Benlar's hair.

Benlar brushed them off before straightening his body and climbing up. *Where did you move her?*

I told them she was in Maringow. No one questioned me. From the beginning, I watched over her as she slept, but on the trip, there was an accident. She wasn't supposed to wake up.

Avia stopped above Benlar. The light of his flashlight beamed through her thin teal fin.

I held her as she cried in my arms. She was a baby, Helo continued. *Her tiny hand wrapped around my finger. Our crew managed to repair her hibernation chamber, but I couldn't put her back in that coffin.*

Benlar's heart ached for the merman. A moment passed. He knew Avia and Helo were having their own conversation he wasn't privy too. *There's no way Thessa would just allow you to take her.* Benlar broke the private conversation. Their progression ascended once again.

They didn't. There was a price. Helo's voice was strong again.

What did you do? Benlar asked.

I did what was necessary to keep her a secret, Helo answered. *No more. We need to focus on finding her.*

In the silence, Benlar wondered how many died so Mli could live.

The *Clíodhna* rocked in the high tide near the sandy beach. Aidan paced his deck. Being close to land made his fingers twitch. By morning the ship would be beached, and they would be unable to sail if trouble arose. But if he wanted to stay in front of the Navy, this boat needed to be stripped of anything that slowed it down. Aidan gave the order to clean the hull at sunrise. As soon as the task was finished, he wanted to be back on the open seas.

After dinner with LaValle, Aidan had marched back to his rowboat and had rowed back to his ship. Thomas and two of his crewmembers stayed on land. Sleep evaded Aidan as he mulled over Thomas and LaValle's interactions. Mr. Corwin was free to speak his mind to whomever he wished. But Aidan couldn't force him to come back to the ship. The line was drawn. The risk, taken.

Silver clouds covered the stars and sealed in the heat of Madagascar. Aidan's boots thudded with each step. The day was easier than planned, but he couldn't help fear tomorrow and any new demands that might come from Captain Augustus LaValle—he was a pirate after all.

The perfume of the forest wafted over the ship. Animals of the night called to each other, hunting their prey. This world's fearsome beasts were nothing compared to the creatures that rose from the depth of the sea.

Aidan leaned against the rail, inhaling the salty air. If Jocelyn was a mermaid, why would she want to come back to him? Would she really want to live on land? If he were given the choice of land or sea, he would choose the sea. Being on board a ship was peaceful, magical, unlike the chaos of land. He pulled off his hat and set it on a barrel next to him. His dark hair fell in his eyes. Brushing his hand through the strands, he moved them out of his face.

He knew he loved her, but was he being selfish wishing she would return and stay above for him?

"Captain?" a small voice asked.

Aidan turned to find George standing behind him.

"Wot are those sounds?" the boy asked.

"Tigers or lions."

George's face perked up. "Really?"

Aidan turned from the ocean to look at the dark forest's line of trees.

"I've always wanted to see a tiger," the boy confessed.

"I've seen a stuffed one, once."

"Yeah? Did ye touch it?"

Smiling, Aidan nodded. "I thought it would've been softer."

"In the orphanage, I met a boy who saw a real tiger and touched it."

"Is that so?"

George grinned, displaying two overgrown front teeth. "He said the trick is never to be afraid. The worse anything could ever do is kill you."

Aidan picked up his hat. "Your friend is wise. Was he adopted?"

The boy shook his head. "No. He only came at night when we told each other stories of how we were going to leave."

Looking down at the child, a ting of sadness crept over

Aidan. Even for a brief moment, this boy had a family who loved him, even if it was only other lost boys and imaginary friends to remind him he wasn't alone in this cruel world.

"What was your story about?" Aidan asked.

George looked up at his captain. "I wanted to fly away with Peter."

The mermaid stretched her back as she rolled her neck, her auburn hair cascaded around her shoulders. Jocelyn had seen this woman a hundred times staring back at her in the mirror, but now she was afraid of her own reflection.

"You are me."

The merrow shook her head. "I am Keto. They will never let you go unless you allow me to help you," Keto sang, her voice a sweet lullaby.

"Where were you when I needed you? Why are you here now?" Jocelyn asked.

The mermaid blinked. "Sleeping. You woke me when you were not strong enough."

"I know what you want to do," Jocelyn said. She lay back in the surrounding waters, staring up at the vivid sky.

"That is because you want it too." Keto lay beside her and took her hand. "I won't hurt them."

"You're lying," Jocelyn retorted.

The mermaid leaned over and kissed her forehead. "Sleep, child. They can hear you."

CHAPTER 31

The crawl space opened into a round room with a point at the top. Benlar swam away from Avia and Helo, welcoming the space. There was no way in or out other than the way they'd come.

Where are we? Avia asked, glancing around the room.

Helo pulled out his crossbow and armed it with an arrow. *In a dome above my old chambers.*

Benlar followed suit, unclipping his weapon and adjusting it to fighting mode.

The medical clinic is four doors east. We might have to fight our way in, Helo informed the group.

How long has it been since you were here? Benlar asked.

Eighteen years.

Things could have changed.

Helo shook his head. *We don't like change.*

What do we do when we have her? Avia prepared her bow.

If it's easy, we come back this way, Helo said.

Nothing's ever easy. Avia's voice shook.

No, my dear, it never is. We'll swim out from the balcony and head east. Below the statue of Ther-sa, there's another way back to the underground tunnel.

Do you have a statue too? Benlar couldn't help but ask.

No. Inam wanted to remind me who's in charge, Helo answered, uncovering his blade. *Once we leave this room, stay behind me.*

He grabbed his black braid, pulled it away from his scalp, and sliced it with his knife. He handed the knife to Avia. She cut his hair in layers down to his chin.

Benlar studied the thousand-year-old young merman's face that he shared with the merman on the posters he saw growing up. Helo looked identical to Inam.

Helo grinned at him. *He's my twin brother.*

I can see that.

Let's hope everyone believes you're him, Avia added, returning Helo's knife. *Let's go get my granddaughter.*

Helo kissed his wife. *I love you. Remember that.*

Always, Avia said, caressing his face.

Helo swam to the middle of the room and lifted a square tile from the ground. He peered around the room. *It's empty,* he said before dropping in.

Avia and Benlar followed him into the Cathedral.

Coldness surrounded her. The room smelled of wet wood and dried rose peddles. Jocelyn lay on the floor, staring up at the clay roof.

"Do you remember?" Keto asked, mirroring Jocelyn as she lay on the ceiling.

Jocelyn shook her head.

"But you do."

The mermaid tilted her head, inhaling the past.

"Memories are absurd creatures, disappearing over time,

or in your case, until a small reminder sends it fluttering back." Keto swam above Jocelyn. Her hair drifted down over Jocelyn's, blending together. "I am your reminder."

The creature grabbed Jocelyn's face and turned it toward the corner, to a bed on the floor where a child slept. Tears seeped from the girl's eyes as she dreamed.

"Do you remember your dreams?" the mermaid asked.

"No."

The small child opened her tear-soaked eyes and stared at Jocelyn. The blues raged in the girl's eyes as rain pelted the roof.

A door flew open. Fear washed over the girl and into Jocelyn as two men rushed toward her. The taller man wrapped her in his arms and held her on his lap as they sat on the bed. The other pressed a wood cup to her mouth, forcing her to drink. The child's blue eyes turned black as they rolled back, and her eyelids shut—her body limp. A tear ran down her cheek.

"Do you remember?" Keto asked again.

Jocelyn nodded. "I dreamed they were all drowning."

Sailors scraped away barnacles and replaced rotting boards from the hull of the massive ship beached in the low tide. The morning's cloudy sky flicked droplets from the heavens. A warm storm was blowing in.

A table had been brought from the merchant ship and placed on the beach. Aidan stood over it, studying maps spread on top. A heavy Ramsden sextant held the navigation charts from flying away in the increasing wind.

"Have you set your course?" a woman's voice asked.

Aidan recognized Adalene's voice and turned. Her blonde ringlets bounced around her face as her heels sank into the sand, leaving footprints behind her. Thomas's arm was linked with hers.

Glancing between the two, Aidan frowned. To mess with the king's daughter could bring war. He hoped Thomas was smart enough to realize the dangers attached with the girl.

"Aye," he said, turning back to the maps. "We'll leave tomorrow, once your father provides the trade."

Adalene dropped her arm from Thomas's and stepped to Aidan's side. "Oh, don't be daft. You should stay longer than a mere two days. Rest, my family insists."

Aidan straightened, towering over her. Her baby-blue silk dress drifted with the current of wind. Embroidered white flowers covered the bodice of her gown. Aidan couldn't imagine the price of such a garment.

"I don't think that would be wise. But thank you for the gracious invite. Now if you don't mind, I have a lot of work to attend to." Aidan bowed before returning to the table.

Adalene puffed, reminding Aidan of a child ready to throw a tantrum. "Then I insist you lend me Mr. Corwin. I fancy a new conversationalist."

"I would be honored," Thomas answered.

"No." Aidan's voice left no room for argument.

"No!" Adalene exclaimed.

Her surprise let Aidan know the girl was used to getting her way. "No. There is much to be done, and Thomas is needed here."

Adalene glared at him. "My father…"

"Would agree," Aidan finished for her.

The roar of the waves crashed onto the sand.

"I liked you more as a boy."

Thomas placed a fist on the table and leaned into the wind. Dark clouds covered the sky, darkening the day. "It won't hurt for the girl to escort me about. Mingle with the locals."

Aidan pushed Thomas's hands off a map and began to roll the delicate paper as a few scattered raindrops fell. The smell of wet sand permeated the wind.

"If you can't take orders, Mr. Corwin, you might become a local."

"I think I might like that." Thomas grinned, staring at the beached ship.

Thick raindrops imprinted the sand as more and more fell.

Thomas grabbed a map, rolled it, and handed it to Aidan. "You should cover them before the ink runs." He reached out his hand to Adalene. "I would like to see more of your island, my dear."

Adalene giggled, taking the offered arm and linking hers with his. "We might want to find shelter."

Before the two could walk off, Aidan grabbed Thomas's arm and leaned close, the maps pressed to his chest. "Do not do anything foolish. Remember whom you're challenging," he whispered into Thomas's ear.

"I'm not challenging anyone, Captain. I'm just removing the lady from the weather," Thomas said, brushing Aidan aside. "Shall we?"

Wrapping his coat around the maps, Aidan watched them walk toward town—arms linked. Rain spilled over his coat, threatening the maps within. "Damn it."

The storm raged over the sea, mirroring what was to come if Thomas had his way.

CHAPTER 32

Gold trim decorated the hallway, matching the chandeliers dangling above. They passed two unguarded, tall doors, but the third was surrounded. Soldiers glanced at Helo then bowed as he swam by—his head held high, declaring his authority. Avia swam on his right with her bow angled low.

Benlar wondered how many non-uniformed guards the Descendants had roaming the grounds, unsuspected.

Helo waved his hand as they approached the fourth door. The guards parted, allowing them access to the medical clinic.

Panic tore into Benlar as his appearance continued to be unchallenged by the seven armed mermen. He held tight to his crossbow but did not raise it.

Turning the silver nob, Helo opened the door to find men and women rushing around the large room. Hibernation chambers lined the floor, each one connected to a metal tank by rubber tubing.

The door closed behind them, leaving the army without.

Looking over Helo's shoulder, Benlar spotted Mli lying on a porcelain medical table on the other end of the room. A merman sat beside her with his back toward them.

The medical staff stared at Helo, then at the merman,

halting their rushed jobs.

Leave us, the merman said, holding Mli's hand.

The staff disappeared without another order.

Benlar raised his weapon, but Helo placed his hand on top of the bow and pushed it down, shaking his head.

Brother, Helo said.

Inam turned, facing the group. *I'm glad you remembered your way home.*

It's hard to forget.

Inam bowed his head at Avia. *You look well. I assume my brother is taking care of you.*

Avia pointed her crossbow at him. *Get away from my granddaughter.*

Shaking his head, Inam drifted from his chair, dropping Mli's hand on the hard surface. *She was never yours. You were just a healer assigned to her who happened to win the heart of a Descendent.*

This coming from the merman who kept her in a box, Avia said.

Inam glared at her. *It was her choice, as I remember my brother telling you over and over.*

Benlar aimed his weapon at the Descendant's head, done with small talk. *Move away from her,* he ordered.

Inam waved his finger. *Put that away. Threats are pointless at this estate. I've already won, and I wish for no one else to get hurt.*

Helo moved forward. *Like my daughter and her husband?*

Inam shrugged. *What do you want me to say? I'm sorry? Because I will, but if you're to blame anyone, it should be yourself. Of all of us, you knew the risk of taking her.*

Helo swam over the hibernation tanks. *Because I stayed in the shadows as your puppet, stepping in as needed to keep your power over this world? Or because I watched her sleep for centuries as dust collected around her?*

Inam rolled his eyes. *Stop being dramatic. We all watched her.*

But you have seen what she can do. Become. And still you took the risk.

We promised her, Helo said, pointing at the sleeping Mli.

She killed thousands. We would have promised her anything.

There is more good in her than you give her credit.

Inam's face contorted as anger filled his eyes. *Where was the good when she brought the ocean raging down on Atlantis? Where was the good when my son drowned? The girl you saved is nothing more than a monster who needs to go back into her cage.*

I won't let you do that! Benlar shouted. His finger rested on the trigger, ready to pull.

Threaten me again, boy, and those guards will descend into this room and pull you apart.

Mli's head moved to the side. Benlar glanced down at her, then to the IV inserted in her arm. Her blood drained into a clear bag.

What are you doing to her? Benlar asked, taking note of eleven full pouches of blood on a counter.

What they have always done, Avia stated. *Drain her, then regrow her to do it over and over again.*

If you're going to be righteous, why are you still a mermaid? Or were you keeping her for yourself? You do appear younger than last time, Inam said, petting Mli's black hair.

Don't touch her! Benlar ordered.

Inam turned and locked his eyes on Benlar. *How dare you think you can tell me —?*

Before he could finish, an arrow sank into Inam's thigh. Startled, he flung back, hitting the table. Mli's arm rolled over the edge.

We don't have time for a show, Avia rebutted.

Benlar glanced at Avia, still pointing her empty crossbow.

Avia! Helo yelled.

Inam steadied himself. *Guar—* he began to call, but his

speech faded as he slumped over.

Benlar lowed his weapon. *What did you do?*

She poisoned the tip, Helo answered, swimming to his brother.

I gave us a way out, Avia added, darting toward Mli.

Gravity released its grip on her, and Jocelyn floated up. Her head was light, and her world spun around her—faster and faster. Keto's blurry image dissolved into a black silhouette.

"You will never be one of them."

Jocelyn closed her eyes. "I know."

The mermaid reached for Jocelyn. "When you wake, I will be with you. I will protect you."

The soft touch of the Keto's fingers on her face woke Jocelyn from her drug-induced coma. She stared up at Benlar. His ash-blond hair covered part of his face as he pulled an IV from her hand. Blood stained the water, seeping from the opening in the needle.

Benlar. She raised her hand to his cheek.

Benlar's head jerked toward her. *You're awake!*

A young merwoman swam next to him, peering down at Jocelyn. Her gray hair reached toward Jocelyn.

Grandmother?

My light. Avia wrapped her arms around Jocelyn. *I know you're weak, but you have to find strength just for a little longer.* There was a note of pleading to her voice as she helped Jocelyn sit up.

Benlar swooped her into his arms.

You came for me.

Of course I did, Benlar replied, handing his crossbow to Avia. He scoped out the room. No windows and only one door.

Ready? a voice asked from behind Benlar.

Jocelyn glanced over his shoulder at a motionless Inam and his twin. *Who are you?* she asked.

I'm offended, granddaughter. Do you not remember me?

Grandfather? You're his brother.

Her heart raced. Everyone had lied to her. Even the ones who loved her.

I know you have questions, Helo said, lifting Inam in his arms and holding a blade to his neck. *I'll answer them all when we get out.*

Ready? Avia asked.

Helo nodded, swimming past Benlar as her grandmother opened the door.

Guards pointed their weapons, ready to kill, but the living shield, Inam, restrained them from striking.

Move! Helo ordered, pressing the blade against their Descendant's throat.

The guards looked at each other, obviously confused that they looked alike.

Move, or I will kill him!

A guard in front shifted away from Helo, keeping aim with his weapon. Others followed, and a path formed down the hallway.

Now, lock yourselves into that room. Helo lifted his chin toward the open door behind the mermen.

The soldiers didn't move. Helo dug the sharp edge of the knife into his brother's neck, drawing blood.

Move, the guard in charge ordered. His mermen swam into the room. *You can't escape,* the soldier said.

But we will, my dear boy. Now go, Helo said. *And make sure you lock it.*

The merman swam backward, keeping his eyes locked on Helo.

When the click of the lock reverberated in the water, the group dashed for Helo's old bedroom.

Pressing her head against Benlar's chest, Jocelyn clung to the last of her strength.

Flinging open the door, Helo stopped. Fiar and a cluster of guards waited for them. Helo clutched Inam tighter and faced the impending threat. There was no way out. Everything had been a trap.

He knew you would come back, Fiar's hissed.

Jocelyn lifted her head. *You,* she said.

The memory of this merman holding her mother flickered in her mind. Blood surrounded them as he sliced her mother's throat and her life faded away.

Fiar peered around Helo with his right eye. A patch covered his left. *Whatever you do, do not hurt the girl,* Fiar ordered his men.

Yes, sir, his army said in unison, ready to fight.

You don't want to try to kill me like last time? Jocelyn yelled at Fiar.

Fiar grinned. *You were just a bystander then, but now I know what you really are, and Thessa needs you.*

Tonium drifted in the back. Jocelyn pleaded with her eyes for help, but her friend was gone. He belonged to Thessa.

Benlar wrapped her closer to him.

I'll kill him, Helo said, holding the knife to Inam's throat.

Fiar kicked forward. *No, you won't, Helo.*

Jocelyn's grandfather pulled Inam's head back, preparing to kill, but his hand shook. Jocelyn knew, just as Fiar did, that he could not take his brother's life.

Panic rushed into her heart. They were trapped. She swallowed back the fear. There was something she could do to save them all.

Keto drifted behind the soldiers. Her black eyes glared at each merrow. Jocelyn nodded, reaching out to the mermaid.

What is she doing? Fiar asked, alarm lining his voice.

Keto swam between the soldiers, invisible to everyone except Jocelyn.

"Do you wish me to help?" she asked.

"Yes," Jocelyn replied, the water rushing into her throat, gurgling her voice.

Keto smiled. The water spun around her in a slow ripple, getting stronger with each turn. The force intensified, throwing guards against the wall. Furniture tore from the ground and spun in the whirlpool. The mermaid took Jocelyn's hands.

Stop her, Fiar order.

We can't, Helo said, dropping his brother and grabbing Avia.

Keto leaned down and kissed Jocelyn's forehead.

Benlar watched as Mli's eyes glowed white.

"I'll take care of everything," Keto said, becoming one with Jocelyn.

The dome roof shattered as the ocean blasted through.

Keto pushed away from Benlar, her strength returned. Waving her hand, the sea carried Fiar over to her. Her eyes deflected his fear.

Mli, Benlar called out.

She is gone, Keto said.

Taking hold of Fiar's chin, she pierced her nails into his skin. *You will be the first to die,* she said as the ocean squeezed him.

He bellowed in pain as bones broke.

Jocelyn! Benlar cried out.

Flinging Fiar to the ground, the ocean swept him against the wall. He opened and shut his eye, trying to stay conscious.

She is gone.

Then who are you? Avia yelled over the whistling of the fast current.

Keto conducted the ocean with her fingers as she turned to face Avia. *You know what I am.*

Avia pushed Helo away and swam toward her granddaughter, but the sea created a barrier of thick water. *My light, you are stronger than this.*

Keto shook her head. *No, she's not. That's why I'm here to do what she cannot.*

And you have, Benlar said, reaching out. *We need to go.*

Keto turned her back to Avia and stared at Benlar. *I will not be trapped again.*

No one is going to trap you, Benlar promised.

Wood crashed into each other, sending splinters spiraling around. Avia ducked out of the way of a flying chair.

I want what is mine, Keto said.

What is that? Benlar asked.

I want this world to know who their god is.

The ocean separated from the room, dropping the merrows to the ground. Each one struggled to breathe.

Keto's gold tail split into two and transformed into legs. Her feet pattered on the wet floor toward Benlar. Kneeling, she lifted his face. His chest heaved to retain water, but there was none. She leaned down and kissed him. *Goodbye.*

Benlar watched Avia lift her bow and dip the arrow's tip into a jar strapped to her belt, then take aim. Grabbing Keto, he kissed her back.

I'm sorry, he said as her body jarred into his. He peeked over her shoulder at the arrow protruding there, then at Avia's raised crossbow.

Screaming, she clawed to remove the arrow, but the effects of the drug took hold. Keto fell into Benlar's arms. The water washed back into the room as she lost control. With the last of her abilities, she transformed back into a mermaid as the ocean crashed on top of them.

Dark clouds dumped rain over Libertalia, intensifying the smell of sand and forest. Water flowed from dug-out trenches along the muddy road that led to the heart of the pirate colony. A handful of the crew slipped away as they finished their jobs, leaving the slower hands to work. Slimy dirt slid down Aidan's black boots as he marched into the brothel. The ship was finished, and the tide was rising.

The rain rapped on the tightly woven straw roof, and body heat trapped the humidity in the room.

Aidan spotted four of his sailors gathered around a table, devouring food. He didn't blame them for spoiling their palates. Everyone was dreading Henry's cooking on the long voyage back to Europe. The aroma of pineapple lingered, and his stomach growled. The last time Aidan had eaten was the night before in Captain LaValle's home. With the bustle of maintaining his ship and mapping their route, he'd had no desire to eat, until now.

After he took a table in the corner, young women flaunted themselves around him, offering him more than food. But he shook his head, letting them know there was no need to persist.

They were not going to share a bed. The women parted, in search of another man with a heavy coin bag.

A man with a hump over his left shoulder weaved his way through the crowd with a platter of food and drink. He shoved the metal plate onto the table and handed a cup to Aidan.

"Thank you," Aidan said, fishing out money to pay the man.

The man nodded, his brown eyes fastened to the ground. Aidan could tell he preferred being invisible to the world. A man with no name.

"Have you seen a Mr. Corwin around?" Aidan asked, handing the coins over.

The man shook his head and turned.

"How about Miss LaValle?" Aidan whispered.

Glancing over his shoulder, the waiter nodded.

"Was there a gentleman with her?"

He nodded again and took a step forward.

"Do you know where I can find them?" Aidan questioned.

The man shook his head no. "Let's hope no else can either," he said in choppy English.

Aidan exhaled as the man left his table and hobbled back to his bar. That was just like Thomas. If he could stir up trouble, he would.

Surprised by his own hunger, Aidan devoured the fish and rice within a few breaths. The salted meat lingered on his tongue as he drank his ale. He shifted in his chair and pushed the dish away. He needed to find Thomas before the pirate king did, but the comforts of a good meal and the warm room overtook him. His eyes drooped as he nestled down. He succumbed to sleep, and his head fell onto the table.

CHAPTER 33

The once-beautiful room was torn apart, littered with broken soldiers. A few moaned, but most were unconscious or dead.

Mli still in his arms, Benlar ran his hand to the arrow and pulled it from her back. The drug was effective, and she stayed asleep. Blood fanned out from the open wound.

We don't have much time. Avia pulled herself from the ground and grabbed her crossbow.

Wrapping his arms under Mli, Benlar lifted her as he swam up. *I can't go through the wall with her.*

We need to get to the statue. Come, Helo ordered, leaving his brother covered in wreckage.

Dropping from the open ceiling, Benlar dove for the eight statues, their silver arms reaching for the Cathedral. Mli's head bobbed from side to side and her arms flopped as he carried her.

Avia swam at his side, her weapon drawn. No one looked at them but at the rubble drifting down from the destroyed tower. Most of Thessa's guards must've been in the room when Mli lost control, and the ones on the street helped the victims struck by destruction.

Helo's black tail kicked the water as he showed the way to Ther-sa's statue. The Descendant's silver likeness towered over the buildings surrounding her, tail curled up as her blank stare focused on the city.

As Benlar dove, Mli shifted forward, and he squeezed her tight against him. His heart raced with her nearness, and his arms trembled. She had changed in front of him into something he could not understand. The power he saw her wield frightened him to the core. The sweet Mli he loved and knew was not in that room, but something dark had possessed her. Evil. Being hunted by Thessa didn't scare him anymore. It was the thought of Mli waking.

He shook his head, trying to grab hold of his mind. He needed to get them to safety. They needed to get out of the city.

Merpeople darted toward the Cathedral, racing past them. Helo swam behind the statue. *This way!* he yelled.

Benlar followed with Avia covering his back.

At the base where the heavy statue sank into the sand, Helo dug. His hand scraped against something hard, and he brushed the remaining dirt away, revealing a round door with the same symbol of the tree and star as his home and Laza's lab.

Pulling a key from his utility belt, Helo unlocked the door and flung it open to a dark tunnel. *Go!* Helo ordered Avia.

She flicked on her flashlight, then swam in. Thankful for the large width of the door, Benlar slipped in next as he pressed Mli to him. Avia's light darted around the cavern as she swam deeper into the underground tunnel.

The click of the door's lock allowed Benlar to breathe. He turned to face Helo, but the merman wasn't there.

Where is he? Benlar asked.

Covering our tracks, Avia answered without slowing.

Should we wait?

No, he'll find us.

Benlar focused on Avia's light leading the way and swam.

Piean picked at the rubber on the steering wheel. Hours passed, and her fear slipped into sadness, then anxiety took over. She looked at Laza, who sat in the back holding tight to his gun. This merman was not made for adventures, but a lab where he was in control.

She hummed in her head, trying to calm her nerves. They had to be safe, she told herself over and over. Benlar was smart. He would be safe.

A knock on the hatch echoed in the belly of the ship, making her and Laza jump.

Let me in, Helo ordered.

Piean dashed to the door, opening it. Helo swam in.

What happened to your hair? Piean asked.

Are they here? Helo asked, searching the small space.

No. You're the first, Laza answered.

Helo grabbed Piean's shoulder. *Turn the ship to full power and be ready. When they enter, go.*

What happened up there?

Helo blinked. *We lost her.*

Who? Piean asked.

Do you remember how to get back to my home?

She nodded.

Good.

The door flung open.

Is she awake? Helo shoved Piean into the driver's seat. Piean pulled a lever, heating the engine and releasing steam.

No, Avia answered.

Helo held out his arms, and Mli's limp body slid through the door and into his arms.

Benlar followed. *Where were you?* he asked Helo.

There's another way out.

How many tunnels do you have? Benlar asked, taking Mli from him.

Relief washed over the submarine as Avia locked the door behind her.

Too many to count, Helo answered, taking his wife's hand. *Drive, Piean.*

The girl backed out of the mined tunnel, her hand firm on the wheel, keeping it straight to avoid the close walls.

Avia grabbed her medical bag and pulled Benlar close. She floated beside him and Mli. Pulling out an IV, she slid the needle into Mli's arm.

Hold this, she said, handing Helo the tubing.

Avia pulled a glass jar and a syringe from her bag. Poking the tip of the syringe into the lid's thin membrane, she removed its gray contents. She injected the syringe into a thick bag full of liquid and shook it before attaching it to Mli's IV.

This will keep her under, Avia said, staring at her husband. *What she did back there...*

I know, Helo interrupted. *I don't know how far gone she is.*

We can't keep her sedated forever.

I know. But I'm not ready, Helo said.

Ready for what? Benlar asked, stroking Mli's black hair.

To send her home.

Muffled voices surrounded Aidan. His blurry vision came and went with each slow blink. Lit torches flickered in the distance as Aidan held his eyes open and whatever they used to drug him began to fade away.

LaValle sat in a high-backed chair, his boots grounded in the dark sand. A bonfire danced between Aidan and him.

Digging his hands into the beach, Aidan picked himself up. All of his men who'd gone to the brothel were tied together. Some were still passed out and others awake. Thomas was among them.

Brushing the sand from his face, Aidan tried to stand, but his legs refused to take the extra weight. He glared up at the Pirate King and his pirates encircling them.

"What is this about?" Aidan asked.

"Well, my dear boy, Libertalia is for pirates, and you are not one of us," LaValle answered. He rolled a gold coin over the top of his fingers. The metal glistened from the light of the fire.

"We had a deal," Aidan spat out.

"There is dee problem. Never trust us. I've taken charge of your ship…"

"What do you want?" Aidan asked as feeling fluttered back into his legs.

The coin stopped moving.

"You would've killed us, unless you wanted something," Aidan added, standing. Flakes of wet sand fell around him.

The break in the storm circled above, and stars shone through dispersing clouds. The fire crackled as LaValle stared Aidan down.

"My daughter."

"Adalene?"

LaValle exhaled his frustration. "She wants us to spare you. Says it's uncivilized, but I can't just allow you to walk away."

Thomas wiggled. "What about my father?"

"He is dead."

"I helped your family escape." Aidan's knees wobbled for a moment, before he demanded control of his body.

"I am truly grateful for that, and that is why you're here." LaValle picked up a pistol from the sand and threw it at Aidan's feet.

"What am I to do with that?" Aidan asked.

"I'm curious too." LaValle waved his hand, and the hunchbacked man untied Thomas and pushed him toward Aidan. "If you can prove you are one of us, den I'll give you back your ship, men, and what you came for. But if not, I will kill each of you. Pick it up."

Aidan stared at his men, then at Thomas. "Are you asking me to kill Mr. Corwin?"

"I want a life, Mr. Boyd," LaValle said, standing from his chair.

Thomas looked at the gun, then Aidan, before darting for the weapon. Aidan grabbed it first, flinging sand into the fire as he aimed. Thomas froze.

"Please. You need me. I have friends that can help us," Thomas pleaded.

Adjusting the weapon in his grip, Aidan looked at LaValle. "You just want a life?"

The pirate king nodded.

He clicked the trigger back, ready to fire, aiming at Thomas's head. Before he released the bullet, Aidan shifted the gun at the hunchback and fired. Thomas fell to his knees as the other man dropped dead.

LaValle's face paled as he watched his man fall.

"If he was going to poison me, he should've killed me," Aidan said, throwing the pistol at LaValle's feet. "I would like my ship and the weapons, now!"

Aidan's hands shook, but he clenched them tightly. He'd killed a man. It didn't break him as he thought it would, and if he let it, it would make him stronger.

LaValle smiled at him. "I've underestimated you, Captain."

CHAPTER 34

Four jolly boats rowed toward the ship, each filled with swords, pistols, and a cannon. Aidan ascended the ladder to the deck of his ship.

Nicholas and the other crewmembers cowered on the floor, surrounded by LaValle's men. The *Clíodhna* rocked with the ocean.

"Took ye long enough," Nicholas said. "These bloody imbeciles 'ave taken our ship."

"No, they have not," Aidan declared.

Drawn swords turned toward Aidan but quickly dropped as someone on the beach covered and uncovered the fire. A sign to release the ship. The pirates backed away from the men.

"Where are your boats?" Aidan asked a pirate wearing spectacles.

"At the bow," the man answered, his sword still in hand.

"Nicholas, ready Captain LaValle's supplies. These men are to bring back the trade tonight."

"Aye," Nicholas picked himself up off the ground.

"We'll need our strongest men at the port."

Nicholas nodded to Aidan. "'Tis good to have ye back,

Captain." He patted Aidan's shoulder. "Markus! Michael! Ready me two crews."

The sailors rushed to their tasks.

Rubbing his hand, Aidan could still feel the pull of the pistol as it released the bullet. The nameless man's eyes rolling back. His face as life left the body. Aidan wondered how long this ghost would haunt him.

Thomas stepped to his side, looking at the full moon touching the horizon. The two stood for a long moment.

"Why did you spare me?" Thomas finally asked, his voice shaky.

Aidan looked at the few stars shining through. "Because I knew your name."

Thomas fiddled with his dirty hands. "Thank you."

Aidan faced him. "Your life is mine now. You will do as I say, and if you cross me, I will kill you."

Thomas held his breath.

"Join the crew. We have work that needs to be done before we set sail."

"Yes, Captain."

Aidan pushed past Thomas, heading for the wheel of his ship. With each step, he shed his past with footprints of sand and water. The bullet had killed two men. Aidan Boyd was buried deep in the sands of Madagascar. He hooked his fingers around the wooden pegs, reminding him of the window's latch in the pub in India. The way the sharp edge of the hook held tight, securing panels from the wind—protecting its home.

His navigator, Adam, took his place next to him. "Where are we heading, Captain?"

"Ireland. I've lost someone, and I'm going to find her. And from now on, I'm to be addressed as Captain James Hook."

Piean drove the Sailfish at full speed.

Laza, Avia, and Helo watched Mli in Benlar's arms. Her chest rose and fell in a gentle pattern.

There it is! Piean shouted, seeing the opening to the cavern. The submarine flew through it. She pointed its nose toward their train.

What do you mean, her home? Benlar asked, holding Mli's hand.

She's not from here. She was never meant to stay, Helo said, his eyes settling on Mli's face.

Laza shook his head. *What will happen to us if she leaves?*

We can't exist as we are once the supply is gone.

You can't be serious, Helo. What you're saying will destroy us. Laza ran his hand through his red, stringy hair.

I know, Helo answered.

The ship fell quiet, other than the humming of the engine. Piean pressed the button and opened the back of the train. Pulling up the steering wheel, she directed the Sailfish inside the locomotive and parked.

Helo unlatched the hatch and swam toward the front of the train.

Piean left her chair and swam next to Benlar. *What happened up there?*

Benlar looked at the girl. *I don't know how to explain it.*

Piean sat against the wall next to him. *Did she do something?*

Benlar nodded.

The train jerked forward. Piean fell against Benlar's shoulder, but she didn't move away.

We should move her, Avia said, holding the IV container to her chest as if hugging a child.

Benlar glanced up at Mli's grandmother. *Will that wake her?*

No. She'll be out for a few days unless I wake her.

Benlar let go of her hand and swam up. *I'll need you to lift her to me. We both won't fit through the hatch,* he said, passing Mli to Avia.

Avia wrapped her arms under Mli's, and Piean swam over and lifted her gold tail to keep it from dragging.

Twenty. Thirty years, Laza mumbled.

What are you talking about? Piean asked him.

The old merman stared at her. *Did you hear them? With what Helo's proposing, I'm not going to be able to de-age again. Twenty or thirty years, if I'm lucky.*

That's enough, Benlar said, swimming past the group and through the door on the roof. His hand dropped into the opening. *Hand her to me.*

Avia swam up, lifting Mli.

Benlar grabbed her arms and pulled Mli through the door. He rested her above the submarine as he repositioned her in his arms and waited for the IV.

Mli's head rolled to the side. Benlar froze.

What's the matter? Avia asked, swimming through the door with the bag.

Her head moved.

That's impossible. There's no way she can wake up. Get her to the car. Quickly, Avia ordered, holding the IV bag as she swam beside Benlar to the front of the train.

Set her there. She pointed to a couch in the entertaining car.

Benlar placed Mli down, folding her arms on her lap.

Avia drifted above her, straightening the IV tube to make sure the drug was getting into her. They both watched.

What are you doing? Helo asked, glancing into the room

from the pilot's station.

Shh, Avia said.

Mli's fingers flinched.

That can't be.

What? Helo asked as Laza and Piean swam in.

She's waking up. Avia pointed to Mli's moving hand. *She's getting stronger. You need to go faster.*

Helo accelerated the train to full speed. The wheels chirped against the metal rails below them.

What will happen if she wakes? Piean asked, taking Benlar's hand.

It depends who's in charge, Benlar answered, interlocking his fingers with hers.

For two hours they watched Mli's body move in a slow progression. First her hands, then her fin. Avia continued to pump her full of the sleeping agent, but it was losing its effect.

We're home, Helo stated, slowing the train.

We don't have much time, Avia said as Benlar lifted Mli into his arms. *Follow me.*

Benlar nodded.

The train stopped with a jerk, swishing the water around them, and the door opened to the large cavern. Avia darted out with her leather medical kit in hand. Benlar kept to her right.

Where are we going?

To the medical clinic, Avia answered Benlar.

What do you plan to do?

Give us more time.

They reached the top of the cave, the door to Helo and Avia's home. She unlocked it and swam in. Benlar and the others followed. The long tunnel seemed to grow longer as Mli moaned. They swam past rooms carved into the earth, some with doors open, others closed.

Here! Avia flung open a door.

Benlar entered the medical room. Avia grabbed a handle on the wall and pulled. A hibernation chamber rolled into the center of the room.

You have your own? Laza's jealous voice asked at the opening of the door.

It is a precaution, Helo said, swimming around the old merman.

Helo pulled back the glass lid.

Put her in, Avia ordered, clearing the shelves of what she needed for the procedure.

Benlar did as told and laid Mli in the casket. He kissed her hand before Avia pushed him out of the way and closed the lid. Locked it with a click.

Mli's eye fluttered open. Panic settled over her as Avia twisted a tube into the chamber.

Pounding her fist on the glass, Mli's black eyes found Benlar's.

I'm sorry, he said, a hard lump forming in the back of his throat.

She scratched at the glass. *Please, don't do this!* Mli pleaded.

Benlar swam forward, but Helo grabbed him. *Don't.*

Mli slammed her fist into the lid, cracking it. The black in her eyes faded to gray, then white.

Mli screamed as Avia turned the hibernation tank on.

THE END

Don't miss the conclusion in

Rising

Book Three of the Sinking Trilogy.

Coming Soon from L2L2 Publishing.

ACKNOWLEDGMENTS

Life is not easy, and writing a book on top of that is damn hard, but with these wonderful people, *Drifting* is not stuck in my mind but is on paper. I want to thank each and every one of you who helped this dream come true.

To Emma, Elijah, Elliana, and Esmae: You helped with requests of endless storytelling during our long car rides. You continue to surprise me with your questions of "what if this happened" that end up finding a way into my books. You fill my world with inspiration and magic that teaches me to grow, not only as a writer, but also as a person. I love you, and you're my favorites.

To my sexy, wonderful, supportive husband, Josh, who owns my heart: I couldn't do this without you. From the beginning of our relationship, and hopefully to the end, we will continue to be dreamers, and our dreams are coming true. Thank you for holding my hand when I needed it.

To Jon and Pauline for hanging out with my kids so I could get another chapter done: Without your support, this book would have taken much longer to finish. Thank you!

To Kathy, Jessica, and Pam for your critiques: You three are godsends! Thank you for telling me what worked and what didn't.

To my amazing friend and editor, Michele: Thank you for loving these stories as much as I do. None of this would have happened without you!

To the reviewers, bloggers, fans, and readers: I thank you for all of your support. I love hearing if you were an Aidan or Benlar fan! This trilogy is for you.

To my parents who always believed I could do anything: Thank you for being my rock. Dad, I would have given up a long time ago without you telling me nothing happens overnight. Mom, even though you are not here, I can feel you and know you are reading my books. Thank you for giving me a magical childhood that fuels me to write.

And last, I want to thank God for giving me the heart to write.

~Sarah Armstrong-Garner

About the Author

Sarah Armstrong-Garner lives in Northern California with her husband and three children, and get this: not only is she an author, screenwriter, and photographer, she also shoots indie films with her husband.

You can visit **www.SarahArmstrongGarner.com** to learn more about her and her upcoming releases.

Sarah loves to hear from her readers! Follow her on social media, check out her website, or drop her a line to let her know what you thought of Drifting. *Happy reading!*

www.SarahArmstrongGarner.com
Facebook: @SarahArmstrongGarner
Twitter: @SarahTwyla
Instagram: @SarahArmstrongGarner

REVIEWS

Did you know reviews can skyrocket a book's career? Instead of fizzling into nothing, a book will be suggested by Amazon, shared by Goodreads, or showcased by Barnes & Noble. Plus, authors treasure reviews! (And read them over and over and over…)

If you enjoyed this book, would you consider leaving a review on:

- Amazon
- Barnes & Noble
- Goodreads

…or perhaps even your personal blog? Thank you so much!

—The L2L2 Publishing Team

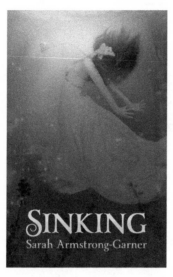

More from L2L2 Publishing

If you enjoyed this book, you may also enjoy:

Candace Marshall hates zombie movies. She hates anything scary, in fact. In his usual, not-so-thoughtful way, her boyfriend surprises her with advanced screening tickets to the latest zombie flick, complete with interactive features and a tour. She refuses to watch it, but it doesn't matter. Horror becomes reality when an experiment gone wrong transforms her peaceful town into a mess of slathering zombies. Thrown together with the only other survivor, Gavin Bailey, her favorite actor and secret crush, she somehow fights her way through the mess, making plenty of blunders and surprising herself with . . . courage? But, just when Candace thinks it can't get worse than zombies, it does.

More from L2L2 Publishing

If you enjoyed this book, you may also enjoy:

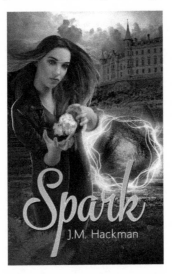

Brenna James wants three things for her sixteenth birthday: to find her history notes before the test, to have her mother return from her business trip, and to stop creating fire with her bare hands. Yeah, that's so not happening. Unfortunately. When Brenna learns her mother is missing in an alternate reality called Linneah, she travels through a portal to find her. Against her will. Who knew portals even existed? But Brenna's arrival in Linneah begins the fulfillment of an ancient prophecy, including a royal murder and the theft of Linneah's most powerful relic: the Sacred Veil. Hold up. Can everything just slow down for a sec? Left with no other choice, Brenna and her new friend Baldwin pursue the thief into the dangerous woods of Silvastamen. When they spy an army marching toward Linneah, Brenna is horrified. Can she find the veil, save her mother, and warn Linneah in time?

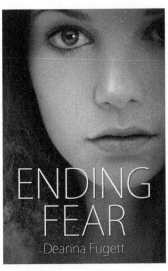

More from L2L2 Publishing

If you enjoyed this book, you may also enjoy:

Leah spends her days scrubbing floors, polishing silver, and meekly curtsying to nobility. Nothing distinguishes her from the other commoners serving at the palace, except her red hair. And her secret friendship with Rafe, the Crown Prince of Imperia. But Leah's safe, ordinary world begins to splinter. Rafe's parents announce his betrothal to a foreign princess, and she unearths a plot to overthrow the royal family. When she reports it without proof, her life shatters completely when the queen banishes her for treason. Harbored by an unusual group of nuns, Leah must secure Rafe's safety before it's too late. But her quest reveals a villain far more sinister than an ambitious nobleman with his eye on the throne. Can a common maidservant summon the courage to fight for her dearest friend?

WHERE WILL WE TAKE YOU NEXT?

Drift into *Sinking*,
Enjoy *Zombie Takeover*,
Discover *Spark*,
Read *Ending Fear*,
and Buy *Common*.

All at
www.love2readlove2writepublishing.com/bookstore
or your local or online retailer.

Happy Reading!
~The L2L2 Publishing Team

About L2L2 Publishing

Love2ReadLove2Write Publishing, LLC is a small traditional press, dedicated to clean or Christian speculative fiction.

Speculative genres include but are not limited to: Fantasy, Science Fiction, Fairy Tales, Magical Realism, Time Travel, Spiritual Warfare, Alternate History, Chillers (such as vampires, zombies, werewolves, or light horror), Superhero Fiction, Steampunk, Supernatural, Paranormal, etc., or a mixture of any of the previous.

We seek stunning tales masterfully told, and we strive to create an exquisite publishing experience for our authors and to produce quality fiction for our readers.

Drifting is at the heart of what we publish: a breathtaking tale with speculative elements to delight our readers.

Visit www.L2L2Publishing.com to view submission guidelines, find our other titles, or learn more about us.

Happy Reading!

~The L2L2 Publishing Team